ON THE TRAIL OF A KILLER

A FAIRMONT FINDS CANINE COZY MYSTERY

CATE LAWLEY

For the most current listing of Cate's books, visit her website:

www.CateLawley.com

For Vegas.

*I cried (a lot) as I wrote this story, but they were sad-
happy tears.*
*How could they be anything else when all my memories
of you are so wonderful?*

*You were the loveliest, sneakiest, cuddliest, and cleverest
of GSPs. Your love of lattes far surpassed my own, and
your ability to sneak a sip without immediate detection
was epic.*

*I know you're out there, stalking squirrels, sipping lattes,
and hunting to your heart's content, because that would
be your heaven...*

And everyone knows that all good dogs go to heaven.

PROLOGUE

The woman of my dreams entered my life two months ago. Griselda Marek. Zella.

I enjoy her company above all others, and the dining has never been finer. Even her scent brings a lightness to my heart. She's a woman I can quietly spend time with, but when she shares the small details of her day, that also brings me joy.

She entered my life at a particularly difficult time, and it was she who helped to pull me from the edge. I'd nearly lost myself in that dark place, but with her by my side I've rediscovered the gentleman within me.

It's my deepest desire to make Zella happy. I owe her no less, since she rescued me from despair and quite possibly death.

My second greatest wish is to help her to find the man of her dreams.

"Fairmont?"

My lady calls.

F airmont!" I called a second time before I saw his chocolatey head emerge from the breakfast room. I hadn't seen him for an hour or so and was starting to worry that he'd slipped out the front door with an incautious visitor, even though I'd put a sign on the front door.

"Have you been sunning yourself?" I rubbed his sun-warmed, silky brown ears as he leaned his head against my leg. I was glad he'd found a quiet spot amidst the bustle and traffic of the estate sale.

Fifty-five pounds of spotted, stubby-tailed couch potato, that was Fairmont. A friend who'd had German Shorthaired Pointers in the past had told me that I should be prepared for some excitement. That after the "honeymoon" period, Fairmont would probably show his true rambunctious colors.

"She didn't know what she was talking about, did she?" I scratched under his chin, and he groaned with contentment.

An older woman in a dated but meticulously kept Chanel suit approached with a determined expression. I recognized her from the neighborhood but couldn't recall her name. She eyed the half-apron tied around my waist with a raised eyebrow. Apparently, it did not meet her sartorial standards.

Omitting any greeting—which failed to meet my *neighborly* standards—she asked, "The piano's for sale?"

I was moving from almost four thousand square feet to nine hundred. I barely had a living room, let alone a music room in my new house. With only the tiniest twinge of regret, I replied, "Yes, it is."

Fairmont heaved a sigh when I stopped petting him. He didn't seem terribly upset to see his home deconstructed and removed via the front door, something I would have guessed a dog would find both confusing and upsetting. Then again, it hadn't been his home for nearly as long as my own.

After inspecting my old Steinway thoroughly, the neighbor returned and offered half the value of the piano. Not for the first time, I wished that my daughter Greta had room for it.

I did a little math. I'd done very nicely on the dining set and my china, and I had no desire to move a piano. Decision made, I countered with a more reasonable sum that was still a fantastic deal.

"Sold," she said. "I'll be by with a check this afternoon."

I pulled a *sold* tag from the deep pocket of my apron. "I hope it brings your family the same joy it did ours."

"It's for my grandson." She shook her head. "He's in a band now, but he still plays for me when he visits. I hope he appreciates the upgrade."

A smile tugged at my lips. He was a musician, so I was guessing he would.

A thoughtful look crossed her face, and she said, "You're too young to be going into a home, so where are you off to?"

A home? A *home*? I was forty-nine! *You better believe I'm too young, you crazy old*—

A cold nose nudged my hand. I knelt, focusing all of my attention on Fairmont. As I ran my hand along his spotted coat, my blood pressure dropped.

Looking at the neighbor I now remembered had always been blunt to the point of rudeness, I replied, in an equally blunt manner, "After leaving my husband of almost thirty years, I should have left his house. It's taken me two years, but I'm finally doing it."

She chuckled. "Good for you. Start fresh." Then she leaned close enough that I was briefly overcome by the strong smell of expensive perfume. "I never did like him."

"Well, I can't say *never*, but you and I seem to have reached the same conclusion in the end."

"Where are you off to? Your lover's apartment?"

I coughed, covering my mouth and my smile. Blunt might have been an understatement. I suddenly recalled her name: Mary.

Mary must have caught a glimpse of my amusement, because she shrugged. "Has to be somewhere small if you're selling everything. And why not with a lover? Some of us divorced ladies have to be getting lucky."

This time, I didn't try to hide my amusement.

"I'm sure that's true." I *hoped* it was, though why Mary had pinned those hopes on me... "Well, I *am* moving to a smaller town and a smaller house, but it will just be Fairmont and me. I'm looking for a new start."

And that was what I got five days later when Fairmont and I pulled away from the now-empty house with a "for sale" sign in the yard.

2

She's afraid.

I can smell the scent of fear. I know that scent—am intimately acquainted with it—but my lady shouldn't smell of fear.

She should smell like the sun and the rain and the sweetest things in life. She usually does. But this car ride has frightened her.

Perhaps we travel to the doctor?

A shudder ripples through me, and memories of antiseptic smells and sharp needles dance in my head.

A glance at the back of the car, filled with all of my lady's favorite items, reassures me that's an unlikely destination. But whatever the cause, my lady's distress is clear, so I try to stay awake to comfort her.

Contrary to my best efforts, the vibration of the car and the scenery whipping by in a blur lull me to sleep.

F airmont and I arrived at our new house two hours later. I took a deep breath as I pulled into the drive, and Fairmont mimicked me with a big canine sigh as he woke from a long nap. I rubbed his ears. Running my fingers over their velvety softness soothed me for reasons I couldn't explain.

My grand, life-changing adventure started two months ago when I adopted Fairmont.

A dog-friendly car had followed shortly thereafter. My ex had picked out and bought the sporty Mercedes I'd traded in. It had been a nice, reliable, fashionable car, but the Grand Cherokee was *my* car, chosen by me to meet the needs of my changing life. I patted the dash.

Fairmont and the SUV had only been the beginning. The changes had snowballed from there.

An estate sale, a house sale (two offers were pending), downsizing from almost four thousand square feet to less than a thousand, moving from Austin to White Sage.

"And this, Fairmont, is our new life." I peered at the little box of a house, with its cream paint and black trim. "We should paint the door. Something fun like purple or red, don't you think?"

He blinked sleepily at me, looking not the least bit enthused about painting.

"Don't worry. I'll do all the difficult parts. You just have to keep me company." As I ran my hand across his spotted coat, his stubby tail wagged, but he stayed curled up in the seat.

According to what I'd read about the breed, Fairmont was a couch potato outlier. The same friend who'd told me that the end of Fairmont's honeymoon period was coming (it had been coming, according to her, for six weeks now) had also been the one to warn me against adopting him initially. She'd predicted that he would be too much for me.

"Good thing I didn't listen to her. Right, buddy?"

He yawned in response.

I shut the car off, but still I sat, staring at the façade of my new home. Opening the car door and walking into the house, that would make this new life official. I shook my head. "You'd think selling the contents of our former home would have made it official."

His ears perked up. I'd swear sometimes that he understood me.

"There's no sunroom, but there's a huge pecan tree in the middle of the backyard with all sorts of squirrels and birds for you to watch." I leaned over and kissed him on the head. His short tail wiggled. I whispered in his ear, "Watch, not chase, okay?"

His ears drooped for just a second, but then they perked up again as he watched something outside the SUV.

I turned to see what had caught his attention and found a woman headed at a good clip toward us. She had a determined look on her face.

Fairmont and I had been parked in the drive just long enough to gather the attention of a Nosy Neighbor.

"It looks like White Sage isn't so different from our neighborhood in Austin." I gave Fairmont's ear one last rub for good luck, cracked the window a bit, then exited the car with a smile on my face.

"Hi," I called out.

The woman who approached looked to be at least twenty years my senior, but she moved with the energy of a much younger woman. She lifted a hand in greeting and, when she was a little closer, said, "Griselda Reed?"

I extended my hand. "I prefer Zella, and I use my maiden name now, Marek." Or, at least, I did as of three weeks ago. "But you have very good information."

That comment made her grin. "My granddaughter's a real estate agent. I'll have a chat with her about her outdated sources. Helen Granger—I live just around the corner. You've caught me on my midmorning walk."

She made it sound like there was more than one walk a day. Fairmont better not be eavesdropping or he'd start getting ideas.

"You can give your granddaughter a pass. The name change is quite recent."

"Just divorced?" she asked, then frowned. "I'm sorry. That's absolutely none of my business." Her gaze drifted over my shoulder.

I glanced back at the car and saw that Fairmont was straining against his seatbelt harness. I latched on to him as an excellent excuse to avoid discussing my divorce. That was a topic my travel-weary self couldn't politely manage, especially with a woman I'd known less than two minutes.

"Do you mind?" I gestured to the car and my impatient dog. "We've been in the car for a few hours. He probably needs a bathroom break."

"Not at all. My departed husband had pointers. And isn't yours a handsome devil?" She was clearly a dog lover, which made me briefly wonder why she didn't have a four-legged buddy to accompany her on her walks.

I opened the door and had to push Fairmont back to get enough slack to unhook him. With my hand firmly on the leash, I stepped away from the driver's door.

He hopped out, but he must have seen a squirrel (or some small, furry creature), because he didn't give Helen even a passing glance or sniff. Without an ounce of hesitation, he galloped toward the house.

Maybe because I was tired from the drive and the start of my new adventure in White Sage, maybe I was just surprised—Fairmont was usually such a gentleman—but either way, he got the best of me. By the time I realized what was happening, my feet were already in motion.

With inertia, fifty-five pounds of doggie leverage, and surprise on his side, Fairmont had the advantage. I wasn't about to let go of his leash, so I ended up tugged along behind, trying not to fall flat on my face.

He came to a shrieking halt when he reached the four-foot chain-link side gate. Literally shrieking.

Nose in the air, paws bouncing from the ground to the fence and back again, barks ringing loud enough to wake the dead, and more determination than I'd ever seen from my sweetheart couch potato: the unexpected commotion froze me in place.

When my brain started firing again, I flipped the gate latch and unclipped his leash. It wasn't like he'd *catch* whatever creature he was intent on chasing, and this way he could get the ya-yas out of his system.

As soon as he was free, he took off like a shot.

I shook my head. Fairmont tended to be a watch-not-chase type of dog. He could stalk birds with a stealthy determination any cat would envy. And barking? Not his cup of tea.

My dog was thoroughly chill...just not today.

Almost immediately, the barking started up again. So incredibly odd. He'd let out the occasional woof, but Fairmont didn't really bark. Well, except for a few well-timed exclamations just as the UPS or FedEx drivers were leaving, enough to make them jump. But that was more a casual reminder that they'd intruded on *his* house, no comparison to the racket he was making now.

Both my home inspector and I had checked the sturdy, though not very attractive, chain-link fence. It was on my list on to-dos to replace it with something more appealing, but there was no doubt it would safely contain Fairmont. I felt comfortable enough to turn my back on him so I could make my apologies to Helen and explain that this wouldn't be a regular occurrence.

But I didn't get a chance to say anything. Something on Helen's face stopped me.

She'd caught up with Fairmont and me just as I'd released him into the yard. Now she was standing just outside the gate, and all of her attention was riveted on the back corner of my yard—and Fairmont.

Raising her voice to be heard over Fairmont's continued barking, she said, "I don't think you should have done that."

Following her gaze, it took me several seconds to grasp what I was seeing.

Fairmont wasn't chasing a squirrel or a cat. In fact, he wasn't chasing anything at all. One hundred percent of his focus was riveted on a stationary bundle in the corner of my new yard.

A bundle of...clothes?

I peered closely, but my feet remained glue in place. On some level, I must have recognized the reality of the situation before it had crystalized fully in my mind, because I had no desire to approach.

A chill crawled up my spine, and I shuddered.

There was a body in my backyard.

4

A body.

In my backyard.

This was not the welcome I'd hoped for in White Sage. Was the universe laughing at my attempt to start over? Maybe, but I was not joining in.

As I refused to laugh in the face of Fate's unfunny plan for me, Fairmont's barks started to come in bursts. He'd bark like mad, then turn to look at me. But then he'd refocus on the body and start barking all over again.

The interminable noise and the stress of seeing my normally calm pet lose his ever-loving mind was making me edgy.

Or perhaps it was the dead man in my yard making me twitchy.

The man-shaped lump had a sprinkling of fall leaves covering him, and I watched as a leaf drifted through the air and landed gently next to him.

Dead, yes, definitely dead.

The context convinced me: the absolute stillness of his body, the accumulation of undisturbed leaves, and something about the arrangement of his limbs. Also, Fairmont had bopped him with his nose, and that hadn't stirred even a flicker of movement.

My new home, my new start, my new life, and this was what I got. Never one for hysteria, I could feel the unfamiliar beginnings of panic creeping in.

But then I came to an important conclusion: a dead man in my yard was a Crisis.

A Crisis was to be handled, not experienced. Every mother knew this. I might not do dead bodies, but I had handled my fair share of crises.

I clapped my hands firmly together and called Fairmont. As agitated as he was, he immediately came back. He looked quite proud of himself. I petted him—he *had* come right back when I'd called —but I couldn't quite manage a "good boy," given the circumstances.

Helen waited while I attached the leash to Fairmont's collar, then said, "You should call the police. Since you're the homeowner, it's best you're the one calling."

Helen Granger also seemed to be the crisis-handling sort. She and I might have to get to know one another a little better, preferably when there wasn't a…

A huff of air escaped my chest.

Plain speaking was best in these situations, even if only in my head, so I tried to imagine the words as just words and not some horrendous event happening to me right now.

Body, corpse, dead man. I repeated the list, but I wasn't so sure that was helping.

In any event, when there wasn't one of those just a few feet away, then I'd very much like to get to know Helen. I'd make sure to make an effort to extend our acquaintanceship once we'd both gotten through this day.

"The police." I nodded in agreement. Definitely someone should call them, and I was the logical choice. "Perhaps you could give Fairmont a potty break down the road while I call it in?"

It seemed a reasonable request, since Helen had remained firmly in control of herself from the first inkling of trouble, and Fairmont hadn't peed since he'd charged out of the car. And if I was misreading Helen's comfort level, it would get her away from the…well, from everything.

She took his leash, but her attention flickered between him and the dead man.

"Maybe you should, you know, *check* first before

you make the call." Her statement was accompanied by a vague gesture in the direction of the body.

"Ah, yes, maybe..." Good grief. What if the man wasn't dead but in some deep coma and desperately in need of medical attention? "Yes! Absolutely. But could you...?"

Helen nodded and clutched Fairmont's leash close to her chest. "I'll stay until you're done."

I didn't make it all the way, just close enough to see his face. Definitely a man and most certainly dead. The wide, staring eyes made it gruesomely clear.

I retraced my steps back to the gate, opened it with careful deliberation, and closed it with equal care. I nodded to Helen and told her she could go. No need for specifics. One person carrying that terrible, wide-eyed, slack-jawed image around was more than enough.

Once the duo were on their way and it was clear Helen had a firm handle on Fairmont, I retrieved my cell from my purse and called 911.

After describing the situation and being told to stay on the line, I explained that I did not feel threatened, that both my dog and I had just come in from a multi-hour car trip, and that we both needed to powder our noses. I firmly excused myself from the phone, to the chagrin of the operator, and then flagged down Helen.

"He watered a few lawns and seems to be done," Helen said as she offered me his leash.

"Actually..." I explained my desire to hit a bathroom and then added, "I refuse to greet the police on my doorstep hopping from one foot to the other."

"It'll be the sheriff, but you're right about the other part. They do like to take their sweet time interviewing witnesses."

Her comment made me wonder how much experience she had with the sheriff's office. Or maybe the town was just that small?

Was White Sage the kind of place where everyone knew everything about anything noteworthy that happened? I'd read about that sort of town in books, seen them on TV, but I'd certainly never lived in such a place. Austin might like to think of itself as a town, but it had been a city for longer than I could remember.

Helen pointed to a neighbor's place a few houses away, and the moment to ask about White Sage's gossip mill and her previous experience with the police was lost.

"Betsy Severs," she said. "Three small kids, and I see her car. She's sure to be home and probably too busy to ask you a bunch of questions."

"Bless you, Helen." I handed her my keys so she could settle Fairmont in my SUV, well away from any flashing lights or brusque strangers. Fairmont had already been through enough today.

She winked at me. Calm in a crisis and kept her sense of humor when a body was right around the corner. My earlier hunch looked to be spot-on. I might like Helen Granger very much indeed—even if she did turn out to have a history with local law enforcement.

5

Hunting, working. I'd forgotten the thrill of it.
There was joy in work.

Different from the contentment I'd found with Zella. In her home, I'd found a soft bed permeated with the smell of my mistress, sun-warmed blankets left just for me in front of a picture window, and leisurely walks with time to smell all of the roses and the grass and the birds and the small creatures that burrowed in the earth.

I would give up work for the love of my mistress.

But...maybe I didn't have to.

6

A fter my quick jog to the Severs' place, I arrived slightly out of breath.

Not that Betsy Severs noticed. She answered the door and, without a word to me or even an apologetic glance, yelled over her shoulder, "Stop that right now, Josh, or no tablet tonight."

A crash was followed by a hollered "Sorry!" and then an ominous silence.

Eyes squinted with suspicion and mouth moving as she silently counted to five, Betsy made me thankful my days as the mother to young children were over.

She turned to me and began to speak as if we'd been having a conversation that had been interrupted. "He plays games on his tablet before bed, so —" She took a step back, quickly surveyed my appearance, and then stretched out her hand in greeting. "You must be my new neighbor."

I smiled, friendly but with a tinge of embarrassment, as I accepted her hand. "Zella Marek. You're Betsy Severs?"

She nodded.

"I hate to impose when we haven't even been properly introduced, but I'm in a bind. I..." I hadn't considered a story appropriate for young ears.

Glancing over her shoulder, Betsy said, "You've got about two more minutes of child-free opportunity here. So make it quick."

Her brusque words were kindly meant, I was sure, because she smiled encouragingly.

"I've just arrived after a long car trip and need to use the restroom." Gulping, I took the plunge. "There's a B-O-D-Y in my yard, and I don't want to go inside until the police have cleared me to."

Her first response was to grin, probably at my lame attempt to disguise the situation. Josh sounded old enough to spell, so fair enough. But that faded quickly, replaced by a perfect O of surprise.

A towheaded toddler appeared just in time to curtail any probing questions, and I hadn't a single doubt Betsy had several. She scooped the toddler up and rested him against her hip. "Right. Say hi, Justin."

The little boy turned wide eyes my way. "I don't like you."

Betsy sighed. "Justin doesn't like anyone right now. Don't take it personally."

I didn't, because contrary to his words, he was smiling at me. Granted, it was a naughty, mischievous smile, but it didn't convey dislike. That little boy looked like trouble. The kind that involved worms on pillows and dirty socks in the oven. I'd had one just like him. I grinned back.

"The bathroom is this way. Don't mind the laundry." She nudged an odiferous pile of clothing with her toe as we walked through the entryway. "Our cleaning lady cancelled at the last minute yesterday. She normally comes in the late afternoon, and I catch up on all the overflow laundry for the week. That's what you've caught me at this morning, since I had to clean yesterday."

That was a new take on the "it's the cleaning lady's day off" excuse. I'd certainly heard it frequently enough. In my old neighborhood, it had been offered when there were a few cups in the sink. More of a token response to any judgment that might be percolating that one's house was less than perfectly prepared for company.

In Betsy's case, I suspected a cleaning lady kept insanity at bay. Three young boys, a husband (there was evidence of a grown male in the household), and all of the mischief and dirt that accompanied such a crew would make a little help on the domestic front appreciated. Just the thought of the bathrooms made me cringe.

My face must have betrayed me, because Betsy winked as she pointed. "The boys aren't allowed in the guest bath."

I was in and out in less than five minutes, and yet I felt like I'd had a much deeper peek into Betsy Severs' life than five minutes might normally allow. I'd caught her unprepared for company. I was sure that was part of it, but it likely also had something to do with the unique circumstances of our meeting. *Bodies bring neighbors closer together*...not a neighborhood slogan I saw catching on.

As I hustled out the door, she waved and said, "Say hello to the sheriff."

If I hadn't been in such a rush, I might have wondered at the amused look she gave me.

When I returned to my house, I joined Helen in the driveway directly behind my SUV. She hung up her phone as I stopped next to her. "You were spot-on about Betsy."

She pocketed her phone. "Three small boys underfoot and her working part-time from home, it's amazing she can put together full sentences. She's a writer."

I set aside thoughts of stinky boys and their piles

of dirty clothes and pondered that for a moment, and just—wow. How could anyone get any work done in the chaos of that house?

But then I remembered that I had my chaos to sort. Those brief moments of forgetfulness had given me a reprieve from the emotional toll finding the stranger had taken, and I was thankful for that. I vowed to get Betsy a night out, even it meant babysitting three rowdy boys.

"I figured we should stay as close to the car and as far away from your house as possible." Helen squinted and leaned close. "In case it's a murder. We don't want to contaminate any evidence."

Murder?

Maybe I'd been thinking it in the back of my mind. I had kept Fairmont and myself clear of the scene. But I hadn't allowed the amorphous cloud of doubts that had floated in my head to coalesce into that particular and very nasty word.

And then Helen had gone and thrown it out into the world.

Murder.

That was when the disbelief and panic hit.

What had I done?

7

J ust my luck, a sheriff's marked car pulled up just as I was doubting my move, my life choices, my existence as a single woman in a tiny town with an apparent dead-body problem...everything.

The deputy was nice enough. I kept reminding myself this as he asked me questions. Really, he was. But he was so *young*. And there was a dead man. On my property. My brand-new-to-me property that was the beginning of my newly unencumbered life.

"Mrs. Marek?" The look on the deputy's face clued me in that it wasn't the first time he'd said my name.

I gave him a weak smile so he'd know he'd caught my attention.

"You don't have any furniture, Mrs. Marek?" He

looked truly baffled by the concept. "It's not coming later today?" Deputy Zapata asked. (I glanced at his name badge to jog my memory.)

He looked down the road hopefully, as if mentioning my nonexistent furniture would make it appear in an equally nonexistent moving truck.

I could have used a friendly face about now. Yelling at sheriff's deputies was frowned upon, I was sure. Not that I'd ever done it, but common sense said it was a bad idea.

But I had no friendly face. No friends at all in White Sage. And Helen, the closest person to a potential *future* friend that I had, had returned home after a brief interview. I wish I knew how she'd managed to keep her chat with the deputy so short, because the repetition involved with my own interview was giving me a headache.

"I've told you twice already. Asking a third time doesn't change the answer." I refused to be embarrassed. There was nothing shameful in divesting oneself of serviceable furniture if it carried the weight of a failed relationship with it. I'd wanted to start fresh, and I was—minus the dead body in my yard. I repeated what I'd already told the young man: "I'm not expecting movers. This is all I have."

I didn't even raise my voice.

A glance in the direction of the car assured me Fairmont was still resting comfortably, and that was when I discovered that another officer had quietly joined Deputy Zapata and me.

He stood a few feet away but well within hearing distance and was making some notes in a small pad. He wasn't dressed in a sheriff's uniform, but in worn jeans, a loose button-down shirt, and hiking boots.

Officer Zapata cleared his throat. "Excuse me, ma'am, about your things—"

"Dave, are you trying to make Ms. Marek uncomfortable?" When the younger man's ear tips turned red, the new man said, "All right, then. Enough with the missing furniture. It's not missing."

I frowned at the man. As annoyed as I was, I didn't think there was any need to embarrass the young deputy. *I* had refrained from exhibiting annoyance, and I was the target of the deputy's mind-boggling confusion.

Dave, Officer Zapata, nodded and said, "Sorry, sir. I remember from last time."

The older man clapped him on the shoulder. "Good man. Now go do something else."

Ah. It looked like Dave Zapata might have ongoing customer-relations issues—or whatever the police version of that might be. Interesting, since I'd have thought making people uncomfortable was rather the point during interrogations.

Which raised the question: was I a suspect being interrogated or a witness being interviewed? Clearly

Helen had been categorized as a witness. Contrary to her earlier comment about drawn-out interviews, her chat with Sage County's finest had lasted all of five minutes.

I supposed the person finding the body usually was a suspect. And while Helen and I had technically found the body together, I was also the homeowner. That sounded like a suspect double whammy. Fiddlesticks.

"Ms. Marek? I'm Sheriff McCord." He waited for me to offer my hand. When I did, he gave me a genuine smile. His hand engulfed my own.

"Zella Marek." I smiled politely. Or I tried to. I'd been here half an hour answering the same questions over and over.

As he released my hand, I realized that Sheriff McCord had mastered the fine art of neither crushing a woman's hand, nor treating it like delicate glass. A difficult skill for many large men.

With regret in his eyes, he said, "I'm sorry that this was your welcome to White Sage."

"I spent some time here with my family years ago, so I'm not entirely new to the area. But I appreciate the sentiment."

He considered my comment, likely trying to root out my local family ties from his memory. Good luck with that, mister. My father's sister had moved to the area after she'd married, so she'd gone by a different name, and she hadn't exactly been sociable.

Nodding in the direction of my car, he said, "Can I have a look at your pointer?"

My heart skittered. "You don't think—" I closed my eyes, tamping down the irrational flash of fear. Of course he didn't think Fairmont had done anything to the man. Where was my head? When I opened my eyes, I found the sheriff patiently waiting for me to finish my thought. "You want to examine him because he touched the body."

The sheriff nodded. "And say hello. He's been cooped up in there a while now."

With so many people present and the care that was being taken, I'd suspected the man in my yard hadn't keeled over from a heart attack. But I'd been trying to avoid the M-word, since Helen's mere mentioning of it had made my head spin.

Now that the sheriff wanted to examine Fairmont for evidence, the thought solidified: murder. In my own backyard, before it even really felt like *my* backyard.

"Nothing invasive," he said. "We just want to have a look to make sure he didn't pick up anything on his coat or feet."

"I understand." Now that the M-word had firmly come to stay, I did understand. I also understood why Deputy Zapata had been so flustered.

When we approached the passenger side of the car, Fairmont stood up and stretched. He must have been keeping half on eye on us. One look at Sheriff McCord and his stubby tail started to vibrate with excitement.

"That's new. He usually only does that for me." I rolled my eyes. "Or food."

"Dogs like me." The sheriff smiled, and that was when I noticed what a handsome man he was.

Not to say I hadn't noticed he was attractive at first glance. I'd catalogued his build (athletic), his clothing (casual and well-worn but high quality), his short, dark brown hair (starting to curl at the ends and due for a trim), his two-day-old stubble, and his lack of a wedding ring.

I was not an unobservant woman. Of course I noticed those things.

But seeing my dog wiggle in joy and McCord's genuine, relaxed smile in response to Fairmont's excitement brought all of those observations into sharp focus: I was attracted to Sage County's hand-some sheriff.

Also, I seemed to be a suspect in a possible homicide being investigated by that same sheriff.

That wasn't awkward, not at all.

8

Sheriff McCord took Fairmont's leash from me and waved a technician over. The tech knelt next to Fairmont and started an examination of his coat, teeth, nails, and pads.

It seemed pretty clear that whatever trace evidence my overenthusiastic dog might have picked up was likely long gone by now, but I guess they had to be careful—if it was murder.

A soft sigh slipped past my lips.

"If you're comfortable leaving him with Tracy"—Sheriff McCord gestured to the tech—"then she can finish up while you walk me through your movements."

"I'll be really careful," Tracy said.

And just then, Fairmont gently nudged her ear

with his nose. The affectionate little nuzzle was also out of character for him, at least with strangers.

I started to apologize for his overfamiliarity, but Tracy was chuckling and whispering words of encouragement and praise. That sold me.

"He's not usually quite so friendly. I guess he has a soft spot for law enforcement." I turned to Sheriff McCord and said, "Lead the way."

"Not at all. I'll follow along. You just do what you did when you arrived." He lifted a hand and waved Deputy Zapata over. "Notes, Dave."

"Yessir." The young man pulled out a notepad exactly like the sheriff's, then trailed behind us.

Once we'd established that I'd arrived around ten that morning, so that Dave could begin an approximate timeline, I took both of them through my introduction to Helen, my sprint to the side gate, and then releasing Fairmont into the yard.

"I didn't think to look in the yard before I turned him loose." I snuck a quick look in the yard and was relieved to see that there was no human-shaped lump in the corner.

"You didn't go into the yard?" the sheriff asked.

"Not at first. I went just far enough to turn Fairmont loose." I pointed over the closed gate at about the place I'd stood.

"Where was Helen?"

"She stayed on this side of the fence." I thought back, trying to recall exactly what had happened. "Fairmont didn't stop to sniff the bushes. He made a beeline for the, ah, the man. He was barking so much, I could barely think. First at the gate and then..."

"Then at the body," Sheriff McCord finished.

"Yes."

"How did you know he was dead?"

Dave's head popped up from his notebook.

I'd checked, but not at first. How did I know?

Because a dead man looks dead?

But that was a flippant, thoughtless answer. I turned my mind back to when I'd first seen the corpse, trying to think about the specific things I'd noticed that had led me to conclude the man in the yard wasn't sleeping off a bender.

Finally, I said, "The yard's been raked recently. The previous homeowners made arrangements to have the fall leaves picked up when they had the house cleaned. And the body, the dead man, had a handful of leaves on top of him. Just a few, like they'd fallen there, not clinging like he'd rolled around and picked them up."

"And from that you gathered that he was dead?" Sheriff McCord's tone was cordial. He didn't seem to be making judgments, just collecting facts.

"No. From that, I gathered that he'd been lying there long enough to have leaves fall on him from the tree overhead. In case you hadn't noticed, it's a little chilly. With the damp on the ground, I'm thinking too chilly to be napping outdoors, especially lying directly on the ground."

He nodded, encouraging me to continue.

"Fairmont was barking loud enough to wake all but the dead. He was also darting in and away and I'm sure poked the body with his nose a few times." I shrugged. "Given all of that information, I thought the man was probably dead."

The sheriff nodded again. "And you could tell from this distance the person was a man?"

"I inferred from his size, and there was also the color of the coat, but no, I didn't know that with certainty until I got closer." I looked at him. "At some point I realized he might be injured— No, that's not right. Helen thought we should check, just to be sure he wasn't injured and was dead like we suspected."

His gaze was fixed on the back corner of my yard. "Did you touch the body?"

"No!" I wrapped my arms tightly around my midsection. "Why would I—" I remembered quite suddenly that the polite plainclothes man I was talking to was the Sage County sheriff. "I'm sorry. No. No, I didn't. I only went close enough to see—"

Examining the image in my head, the dead man's staring eyes, his deathly expression, made me shiver. "Near enough to see that he was obviously dead. I didn't have to get that close, because his face was turned toward me."

His posture relaxed, but there was a grim cast to his face when he said, "You'd be surprised how many people gawk and even touch corpses." He motioned Deputy Zapata closer and spoke quietly with him for a few seconds. When the deputy left, Sheriff McCord said, "Then what did you do?"

"What any sensible person would. I called my dog, fetched my phone, and rang the police."

"After a bathroom break." His mouth had the faintest of curves. I'd say the sheriff looked almost amused, which, strangely, made *me* feel a hint of amusement. It had been a little odd, but given how long I'd been standing out here in the cold, chitchatting with law enforcement, I'd say I made a good call.

"No." I smiled sweetly at him. "The bathroom break was *after* I phoned the police. It's a two-hour drive from Austin, in case you weren't aware. Helen was kind enough to walk Fairmont further down the street to do his business, and I ran over to the Severs' house to use the facilities."

"Staying well away from the yard and your

house, which might have been a possible crime scene."

"Exactly." I nodded decisively. He should be a little more appreciative.

"That was a good choice." He swallowed a grin, then stole away the small compliment with his next words. "And also something the 911 operator would have told you if you'd stayed on the line. And yes, Ms. Marek, I am aware that Austin is a two-hour drive. I lived there for several years." He let the grin he'd been fighting loose. "I'm glad you decided to make the trek and join us in White Sage."

Either he was finding me highly amusing or... Was he flirting with me? He had to be at least five years younger than me, maybe ten.

"I'd rather my arrival had been less eventful," I replied.

"Of course, but you're very clearheaded in a crisis, Ms. Marek." His eyes crinkled at the corners.

If he was indeed flirting with me—and the sustained eye contact said yes—did he flirt with all of his witnesses and suspects? Maybe he was the sort who flirted with everyone, all of the time. Either way, I was overdue a good flirtation.

"I'm a mother, Sheriff McCord. That means I'm a pro when it comes to crises."

Dave appeared with a navy-blue fleece pullover,

curiosity stamped across his face. "Ms. Marek, the sheriff thought you might appreciate a jacket."

I almost asked if I'd really be kept out of my house that much longer that I'd need one, but it was a thoughtful gesture and deserved a politer response.

"Thank you." I accepted the jacket from Deputy Zapata and slipped it over my head. I was immediately enveloped in a pleasant woodsy fragrance, a subtle men's cologne that thankfully held no resemblance to any of the expensive brands my ex favored. The jacket was huge, and obviously belonged to the much larger sheriff and not the deputy. Hugging the warm fleece to my chest, I turned my attention to Sheriff McCord. "I appreciate your thoughtfulness."

"Not at all. Dave can grab you a cup of coffee or hot tea if you'd like."

Deputy Zapata nodded eagerly. The tips of his burning ears combined with his gaze, shifting from me to his boss and back again, gave away his curiosity. Deputy Zapata could use a little help in the subtlety department.

"No, but thank you." I appreciated the kindness, but even more importantly, now I was feeling much less like a suspect. "Oh, and please call me Zella."

The sheriff nodded and, with a less-than-subtle look, checked out my left hand for a ring.

Just like a man to notice the important details so

late in the game. Clasping my hands together, I said, "Divorced."

Wisely, he didn't comment on my marital status, but—with an endearing lopsided smile—he did say, "Call me Luke."

Dave looked up with his pen hovering uncertainly over the pad. The poor boy probably didn't know whether the interview was winding to a close or continuing. And just maybe the sheriff didn't offer up his first name to witnesses with any regularity.

We tidied up a few more details, including the news that I would have to find alternative accommodation for the evening. I'd started to suspect as much halfway through the interview, but it was disappointing nonetheless.

"Please tell me there's a local place that will take Fairmont." As I walked by the front porch, I had the oddest urge to give my house a little encouraging wave, to let it know I'd be back soon.

Luke pulled out his phone and made a call. "Hi. Yes, I'm at work. Can you take someone with a well-behaved dog? Probably just for the one night. Yeah. Absolutely. Thanks, Mom."

Mom? I tilted my head, inviting an explanation.

"My mom runs a tiny house community that includes several short-term rentals."

"And you've just vouched for me."

He shrugged, but his lips were twitching again.

"Do you frequently ship your suspects off to stay with your mother?"

Deputy Zapata snorted and then coughed. Apparently, such questions hadn't been included in his remedial customer-relations training.

9

Luke McCord hadn't argued the fact that I was a suspect, but he had flirted with me. *Probably* flirted with me—it had been a while. But if he had, then I wasn't a serious suspect.

And then he'd gone and sent me off to his mother's.

Wild guess? I was safe from the law for the time being.

The Hiker's Second Home, the tiny house community that Luke's mom Geraldine ran, was only a few miles from my new home. I supposed nothing was far in a town of five thousand and a county only about four times that.

I followed the directions Luke had scrawled in his notepad. As he'd passed me the scrap of paper, he'd mentioned that cell reception blacked out shortly before the turn and I could miss it if I was relying on my phone's mapping app.

He'd also asked if I needed an escort or even someone to drive me. Perhaps I'd been looking especially pale, the curse of the natural blonde, but I'd declined. I was perfectly capable of driving myself and my dog a few miles down the road.

The Hiker was about a quarter mile outside White Sage city limits and only five miles from a good-sized state park, which explained the name Geraldine had chosen.

The lady herself welcomed me with a wave as I pulled into the parking lot. Luke had given me a quick description of his mom, and the tall, athletic woman with a silvery bun, surprisingly youthful appearance, and wide smile fit the bill.

I hadn't expected such a unique combination of outdoorswoman and bohemian artist. She had on a pair of ripped boyfriend jeans worn over colorful tights and paired with a pair of serviceable hiking boots. A long grey cashmere cardigan came almost to her knees and covered a flowing tunic with a wild, fun pattern.

She walked around to the driver's side, hands stuffed into the pockets of her cardigan, and waited for me to exit my car. The moment I set my feet on the ground, she wrapped me in a warm, tight hug. The kind that told you the hugger really meant it.

It took me a moment to recover from the surprise, but then I hugged her back. There was a brief sting of tears in my eyes when I realized it had been a long time since someone had offered to comfort me just because I'd had a bad day. And make no mistake about it, that was exactly where this hug was coming from.

She stepped back with a final pat on my arm and shook her head. "What a way to be welcomed to a new town. I'm sorry for that. But at least you know better days are coming."

My vision was still a bit blurry from the unexpected bubble of emotion, but her dry comment startled a laugh from me. "That is an excellent point." I looked over my shoulder to find Fairmont still curled in the front seat, awake but not in any hurry to escape the confines of the car. "Thank you for letting me stay on such short notice, especially with my extra cargo."

"No trouble at all. We're not fully booked, so I'm glad for the business. And since my son says he's well behaved, he can be responsible for any repairs your dog racks up." She added the last part with a gamine grin. "Now, how about a quick tour before you get settled in?"

Since Fairmont seemed content in the car, I

cracked the window slightly and left him huddled in a snoozy ball in the passenger seat.

There were ten cabins clustered in one area. Each was a tiny home and equipped with a bathroom and kitchen. An eleventh, larger building was set slightly apart and had its own parking, entrance, and signage: The Writer's Retreat. Geraldine explained that it had been partitioned into two small studio spaces and three offices, all intended to serve the local creative community, artists and writers alike.

The two businesses, tiny house rentals and studio space rentals, seemed an interesting combination, and I said as much to Geraldine.

"It's a small town, so everyone has several irons in the fire and is hustling for their dinner. The studio rentals even out the seasonal spikes I experience with the hikers. The meeting room rental helps with that, too. You can't see it from here; it's behind the studios."

"I mean, a conference room? Outside of town? Who would have thought?"

"Ah. That's a bit of story. I built the meeting room after a few visiting writers asked where they could find a conference room in town. There wasn't one, and I figured they couldn't be the only ones looking for a meeting space. But then—surprise! I rented it so frequently that I turned around and invested in the studio spaces. Now I've got regulars in their own dedicated spaces with a waitlist."

All of that, right here in the hill country, at least two hours' drive from a decent-sized city. I couldn't believe she'd made it work, but the place was obviously thriving.

"I love it," I said. "The entire property is gorgeous."

"And you haven't even seen your cabin!" But she smiled brightly, and I could tell the compliment pleased her.

The similarities between her and her son couldn't have been plainer. The smile, the charm, the engaging blue eyes with the generous laugh lines —just like Luke McCord.

She touched my elbow and gestured toward one of the tiny homes. "This way. I'll get you settled into your cabin." She paused. "You know, one of the best things about this place is all of the interesting people I meet."

Said with a straight face. She was good.

I murmured my agreement while simultaneously avoiding any mention of the various reasons I might make the cut as "interesting." There were several: making her son's murder suspect list (even if I was at the bottom), discovering a dead man, or maybe she'd gotten wind of the no-furniture thing.

We stopped in front of a pretty stone cabin.

Geraldine pulled a key from her pocket and unlocked the front door. "Here we are." She opened the door but didn't step in. "You'll find some registration paperwork in the kitchen. When you have a moment, go ahead and fill that out."

I accepted the key she handed me and poked my head inside far enough to spot a clipboard on the butcher-block counter in the minuscule kitchen. "Got it."

"I'm right over there if you need anything." Geraldine pointed to a larger yellow cabin at the back of the property. Perhaps five hundred square feet versus the three to four hundred of the remaining cabins. "And if you can't find me and need something, the green one next door is Hank's." She waved at an older gentleman sitting on the porch of the green cabin. He tipped his John Deere ball cap at us.

"I'll leave you to it, then." She gave my shoulder a reassuring squeeze and then walked briskly away.

She seemed to have an excess of energy, similar to Helen. Maybe it was something in the water or the air. Whatever it was, I hoped it was catching. My new life plan and I could use a little invigorating. Finding a body in a yard that hadn't even begun to feel like my own was having the opposite effect.

Suddenly exhausted, I eyed the full-sized bed tucked cozily into a corner and decked out with a fluffy comforter and several throw pillows. I so badly wanted to sink into its warm embrace and hide from life.

But Fairmont waited.

Thank goodness for Fairmont.

My life is filled with love.

Zella tells me she loves me with everything she does. The cuddles and companionship, my full belly, and so, so many sniff-filled outings.

Does she know she's loved?

Does she know I adore her? That she is loved best?

More than cuddles, more than kibble, more than chasing the teasing tails of squirrels?

I'll do everything I can to let her know, because she's my everything.

F airmont and I settled into the cabin nicely. It was so comfortable that the two of us curled up on the bed and read for a few hours.

Well, I read.

Fairmont rested his head in my lap and stared adoringly before falling asleep. His gentle snores were familiar and surprisingly soothing.

Apparently, escapist literature was the balm I hadn't known I'd needed. Once I'd started reading, images of a certain dead body faded from my mind's eye, replaced with fiery dragons, wicked witches, and an adventure I knew would come to a satisfying conclusion.

No murder mysteries for me today.

The story and Fairmont's warm body nestled

close to mine had lulled me into such a state of relaxation that the ring of my phone made me jump.

I scrambled to grab my e-reader before it fell off the bed, and then I had to reassure Fairmont that no monsters had attempted to devour me. Poor guy. I'd woken him from a rather deep sleep with my panicky movements.

Out of breath and more than a little annoyed (however unjustly), I answered my phone. "Hello?"

"It's Helen. We have to meet. I have news about your dead body."

My dead body? Wait...what? And then I had an unpleasant premonition of my future in White Sage, forever remembered as the lady who found the dead man in her yard.

I wasn't staking that claim. In fact, I'd have to find a way to distance myself. I wasn't completely oblivious to how small towns operated, and it looked like damage control needed to be a priority.

And how did she have any news? I glanced at the digital clock on the stove and found it was late afternoon, all of six hours since the discovery.

My silence didn't discourage her, though, because she said, "And you can tell me what the sheriff had to say. Everyone's saying how he's sweet on you, so he must have given you some inside information."

Sweet on me? Did Helen's generation talk like

that? Maybe it was a small-town saying. But if town gossip had Luke "sweet" on me, then perhaps I hadn't imagined that mild flirtation. I'd only been divorced two years and hadn't spent either of them dating. My dating instincts couldn't even be called rusty. More like atrophied.

It figured that the first romantic spark I'd had in ages was with a man who happened to be investigating a murder on my property and had included me amongst the suspects.

"Zella?"

"Yes, I'm here." I settled back against the headboard, and Fairmont curled into a ball once again beside me.

"Well? Don't keep me waiting. I'm old. I might die from the suspense."

Which made me chuckle. Helen was as spry as—I glanced at Fairmont—as Fairmont stalking squirrels. That I could laugh at the mention of death made me want to hug Helen. Since she wasn't here, I opted to answer her nosy Nelly questions instead. "No idea why you think the sheriff has a thing for me, but he certainly didn't share any insights into the case. He asked me a few questions and sent me off. That was it."

"Um-hm. Sent you off *to his mother's*." She didn't linger on that particular detail—thank goodness, because perhaps that was a little odd. Instead, she switched tacks entirely. "We need to meet to discuss the investigation."

Alarm bells rang, but I replied, calmly enough, "I'd be happy to meet with you, but I truly don't have any information."

"If you're worried the sheriff will decide you're mucking about in his investigation—don't. We're just going to have an innocent little chat."

Good thing she couldn't see my face. There was no hiding my disbelief, because that was a whopper. Her eagerness alone made that clear. "I'm not sure that's a great idea."

Helen snorted. "If anyone should be worried, it's me. It's not like he would put you in jail before he's had a chance to ask you out to dinner."

Which elicited yet another laugh. Maybe I should meet with her. She was doing almost as much to increase my good humor as Fairmont. I rubbed his ears, and he groaned in appreciation.

"Laugh all you like, but that man's been single for longer than anyone half as handsome has the right. If he's showing any interest, you better believe he'll be knocking on your door when this mess is cleared up."

"Aren't you so sweet." Which was one of a handful of my mother's stock replies when she'd been at a loss for a polite response. I was turning into my mother, and all it had taken was a divorce, a move, and a murder.

Helen lowered her voice, and her playful tone turned serious. "We need to meet, and it's not just about some town gossip. Please," she whispered. "Before something bad happens."

Fairmont must have sensed my distress, because he butted me with his head and gave me an intent look. I resumed his ear massage and immediately felt better. In a calm voice, I asked, "Are you saying I'm in some kind of danger?"

"What?" She sounded confused. "No." But before I could exhale a sigh of relief, she said, "Not you, your dog. Fairmont."

I clutched his brown head close to my leg. He didn't protest, but he looked up at me with worried eyes. Relaxing, I scratched his neck and sent him a silent apology.

She was probably a little loony—not that she'd seemed that way earlier today—but that had to be the case. Why would Fairmont be in any kind of danger?

But the doubt had been sowed, and the thought of something happening to him made my heart hurt. "When should I come by?"

"What?" she hollered. "Not here!"

With my cell held a good inch from my ear, I asked, "Where, then?"

After a brief pause, she said, "The Drip. It's only a ten-minute drive from Geraldine's."

I agreed to meet her, even though I hadn't a clue what she expected me to know or what Fairmont could possibly have to do with any of this.

She told me to be sure and bring Fairmont and ended the call.

I stood for some time staring at my phone. Fairmont bumped my hand with his nose.

"Right. We need to get a move on, don't we? Oh, Fairmont, what have we gotten ourselves into?"

My lady is worried.

She's been worried since we left the big house, but this is worse. Since I found the man, so much worse.

Should I not have found the man?

She gave me scratches and pets, but she mostly now seems scared.

H elen hunched close and whispered, "It's murder."

Her demeanor, desire to meet at a neutral location, and now her declaration all pointed to a flair for the dramatic.

Granted, I'd reached the same conclusion: murder most likely *was* afoot. Luke hadn't come out and said it, but all signs pointed to the dead man's end being an unnatural one.

Except Helen was talking about a different death altogether.

"If my little terrier Ace were still alive, he'd have made his way home. It's murder for sure."

The Drip had a large outdoor seating area, which was why Helen had chosen it. The first thing she told me when I'd arrived was that I couldn't let Fairmont out of my sight.

"And you think the—" I glanced around at the handful of people seated outside. "You think the *situation* from this morning has something to do with your dog's disappearance and your friend May's dog dying suddenly?" I refused to call their possible canine deaths "murder."

"Poisoned."

"You think."

"I'm pretty darn sure. May and I were certain that Sylvester had something to do with it. That man hated dogs. And now he's gone and gotten himself *killed*." She whispered the last word.

Fairmont groaned as he shifted on the ground at my feet. I sipped my decaf latte rather than say what was on my mind: that Helen and May were both grief-stricken, that they'd lost their companions and were looking for sense where there was none, and that Helen was maybe just a bit loony or a closet conspiracy theorist.

"And Sylvester was the man in my yard?" When she nodded, I said, "We don't even know that the *situation* is actually a situation. It could have been an accident or a natural, ah, situation." I sipped my drink before I said something even sillier.

But Helen nodded as if she'd understood every word. "It's been confirmed. My granddaughter—"

"The realtor."

"No, that's Cindy. Her older sister Monica works at the salon on Main Street, and she does Dave Zapata's mother's hair once a week."

"Deputy Dave Zapata?"

Helen nodded. "Dave always talks shop with his mama."

I sighed. "And his mama likes to chat with her stylist." The game of telephone didn't surprise me, but the efficiency of White Sage's network made city gossip look like a game of telegraph in comparison. It hadn't even been a full workday. "Is there any information on the exact nature of the *situation*?"

"The nature of the..." Her brow wrinkled then cleared. "Oh. Yes. Pruning snips through the heart."

My eyes bugged. Perhaps bugged was a strong word, but my eyebrows felt like they were trying to meet my hairline.

That person-shaped lump in my yard had been a man, and someone had plunged a pair of gardening snips into him with enough force to pierce his heart.

That was a heap of anger. And it all happened in *my* brand-new backyard.

How was I supposed to start my new life when an unsolved murder was all tangled up with my new beginning?

What had been a tragic event had suddenly become a Problem.

Problems were to be solved. Naturally.

I leaned forward and said in a low voice, "Tell me everything you know about Sylvester, Helen." I pulled out the pretty purple and green journal I'd bought when I'd first decided to move. After flipping past the to-do and supply lists, at the top of a clean page, I wrote: *Sylvester's Situation.*

Over the course of a decaf latte followed by a much-needed, caffeine-rich coffee with hemp milk, Helen revealed the accumulated details of what she believed was an ongoing crime, and she also delivered the scoop on all the parties involved.

Sylvester had been a gruff, not particularly well-liked member of the neighborhood, who happened to live next door to my newly purchased house. An avid gardener, he'd chased away loose dogs from his yard and glowered at any dog walker brave enough to let their pooch tinkle on his roses. He wasn't particularly fond of children either, and was equally likely to chase them away. He was also a dedicated walker and familiar with the comings and goings of pet owners.

Sylvester's particular personality combined with both his dislike of dogs, and the presumed intentional deaths of both May and Helen's furry companions, did look suspicious when viewed from the perspective of a distraught pet owner.

As for Helen's dog Ace, he was a notorious

escape artist. She didn't think there was a yard that could contain him, so she doubted he'd lost his tags and landed mistakenly with a new home. She was certain he'd have found his way home in such a situation. According to Helen, he was a fiercely loyal little fellow and wouldn't miss a home-cooked meal (literally—she cooked every day for him).

Tapping the end of my purple-inked pen, I reviewed the notes I'd made. There was no avoiding it, Helen's conclusions were deeply flawed.

"Go on," Helen said. "Say it. You think I'm a loon."

My increasing desire to turn this fascinating woman into a friend compelled me to speak honestly. "Perhaps for about two seconds when you called earlier, and maybe briefly when you first mentioned canine murder, but generally, no, I'm relatively confident you're not a loon."

Thankfully, she didn't seem offended by my admission. "But?"

I pursed my lips as I formulated a few questions. "First, two dogs—one disappearance and one sudden death—isn't a pattern, so you can't be sure that wasn't a coincidence."

"Ace hasn't just disappeared, but—" She raised her hand to shush me when I would have protested. "Either way, both of our side gates were left wide open."

"Helen," I said. "That's an important fact."

"I beat you here by a good ten minutes, so I'm already pumped up on sugar and caffeine." She jiggled her mostly empty large latte cup. "I might have rushed through certain parts."

"You might have," I agreed. "Anything else you skipped?"

She nodded. "The cats. I've also seen a few lost posters go up over the last month for neighborhood cats. One wouldn't be odd, but I know of three off the top of my head."

An unpleasant sensation prickled at the back of my neck. I rubbed it away and focused on my notes. "Assuming that a pattern can be established and all the pet disappearances in the neighborhood connected in some fashion, then why the concern for Fairmont? If you truly think Sylvester was responsible, then the pets are safe."

We both looked down at my sleepy dog. He'd had a big day so far—a long car ride, his discovery of the body, meeting the sheriff and his staff, checking out his temporary home, and now a coffee outing—so I wasn't surprised he was taking the opportunity to catch a few Zs. He lifted his head off the ground, squinted up at us, then squeezed his sleepy eyes shut with a self-satisfied, contented look.

"Sylvester was the only suspect that May and I

could come up with." She wrapped her hands around her latte. "What if he had an accomplice?"

I gave Helen the same look I gave my daughter Greta when she'd told me that she and Brian Barnard were just studying up in her room.

"Right. I didn't actually think he did." Her shoulders slumped. "Truth be told, I never could believe he'd hurt anyone, human or animal." She sighed. "And I think he used live traps when I saw the pest man come out to his house a year or two ago."

And now I knew why she was so worried for Fairmont. "Which means if there is someone targeting pets, they're still out there."

She nodded, then her expression firmed and she tapped the table with the tip of her index finger. "But I still think that it's all tied together. It has to be." Leaning forward, she said, "What are the chances our little neighborhood has *two* hardened criminals?"

A question that plagued me on my drive home.

While I wouldn't categorize a pet-napper necessarily as a *hardened* criminal—though if the poisoning angle were accurate, that changed things significantly—I did think the possibility of two sets of unrelated crimes somewhat unlikely. The town was small and the neighborhood absolutely tiny. How much mayhem was festering under the shiny surface of White Sage, Texas? As a new resident, I liked to think not that much—which would mean that Helen was correct and all the crimes were inter-related.

And right alongside the question of two master criminals in White Sage (I allowed myself some hyperbole due to the stressful nature of the day), I also asked myself if the Fates were frowning on my new life plan. Not that I believed in such things, but if I *did*...a dead man in my yard was hardly an auspicious beginning.

I turned on the radio, and a song about signs being everywhere streamed through the car.

"No, I don't think so." I turned off the radio and ran a hand over Fairmont's spotted coat. "I don't believe in those kinds of signs. How about you, Fairmont?"

He nudged my hand with his cold nose, which I interpreted as "Hush, and pet me some more." So I did.

By the time I pulled into The Hiker's Second Home, my unease had settled into a niggling little hum in the back of my brain. An improvement over the brass band of discord that had been playing as I'd parted company from Helen at The Drip.

Possible murderers and dognappers aside, White Sage was a wonderful town. Bad things could happen anywhere: in White Sage, in Austin, in any of the three other towns I'd considered moving to. Anywhere.

As I put the Grand Cherokee in park, a county car pulled up next to me. I looked again: not a county car, the sheriff's SUV.

I inspected my manicure and wondered if I was about to be arrested. Perhaps, if I'd paid closer attention on the drive, I'd have seen signs of my impending incarceration?

Luke had come alone. No backup meant no arrest, right? He probably just had a few more questions for me.

That was what I went with, right up until Sheriff Luke McCord knocked on my window, interrupting my intent inspection of my cuticles, and I caught the look on his face.

He did not look pleased.

14

Luke had changed into a uniform at some point over the last several hours. He'd look sexy, if he didn't look like he was about to arrest me.

I rolled my window down when he approached.

He leaned down, and I couldn't detect a hint of softness around his eyes or mouth. He looked very... cop-like. He arched an eyebrow and asked, "Are you planning to get out of your car?"

"Not if you're going to give me bad news." I eyed his cuffs and added, "Or arrest me."

He frowned. "Arrest you?"

I stared pointedly at the cuffs and gun attached to his belt.

He closed his eyes and sighed, and when he

opened them, looked resigned. He gestured to my door. "May I?"

Staying in my car didn't seem to be shortening the visit, so I caved and nodded. He waited for me to roll the window back up, then swung the door open for me.

"No need to look so concerned. I'm not here to arrest you." He frowned at me. "Not yet."

Fairmont barked. It was a single bark and not very loud. Excepting the discovery of dead bodies—which I hoped we'd both seen the last of—Fairmont rarely barked. When I looked to see what the fuss was about, I found him standing in the passenger seat, looking at Luke with adoration and wiggling his spotted butt.

"Traitor," I said affectionately as I walked to the other side of the car. After I retrieved him from the SUV, he butt-wiggled his way up to Luke. "He really likes you."

"Dogs like me."

So he'd said before, but this was a level of excitement Fairmont usually reserved for me.

Luke grinned at Fairmont's enthusiasm and leaned down to rub his ears. "It's not going to work, buddy. You can't butter me up enough to avoid this conversation."

Fairmont sat and then lifted his head to stare at Luke with a quizzical tilt to his head.

"What's happened? Don't tell me: I'm not getting into my house anytime soon."

"Is the cabin not comfortable?"

A smile pulled at my lips as I recalled the fluffy, bright pink towels in the bathroom, the warm duvet, and the cozy pink and green quilt I'd found folded over the back of the loveseat. "I love it. I've even discovered a hidden passion for pink."

"You're in the stone cottage." It wasn't a question, so that pink theme must be unique to my cabin. When I nodded, he said, "Well, I'm glad you're enjoying it, but you likely won't have to stay for long. Your house should be released sometime tomorrow. There's no sign your house was broken into or was involved in any way."

A shiver ran down my spine. "I'm still getting the locks changed."

"Never a bad idea when you move into a new home." He rubbed the side of his neck. "I heard you met up with Helen Granger at The Drip."

I threw my hands in the air. "That just happened! What is going on in this town?"

My outburst surprised him, but he was polite enough to wait for me to compose myself before he continued. "One of the baristas is a friend's kid, and he mentioned to his dad, who mentioned to me that you two were meeting." He rubbed his neck again and squinted. "And plotting."

The skinny kid with the scraggly goatee. I'd bet anything he was the one. If I was still there, I'd reach right into his tip jar and take the two dollars I'd left back out again. Shame on him.

"Is this how things work in White Sage? My every move watched and reported to the *police*?"

"Not the police. They're a tiny, underfunded force, and old Bubba Charleston has a hard enough time keeping up with paperwork and the local drunks. Otherwise, yes. What do you expect in a murder investigation?" And from the earnest expression on his face, he truly was baffled by my reaction.

I clutched Fairmont's leash so hard that I could feel my nails bite into the palm of my hand. "For one, I'd expect the law enforcement agency investigating the crime on my property to inform me that it was a murder."

Luke groaned. "Can we go inside and talk about this? If we're out here much longer, my mom is going to have a conniption."

First, I didn't envision Geraldine as a woman who'd ever had a conniption. Second, I didn't even want to imagine the gossip if I invited Luke back to my cabin. If chatting at a coffee shop with a new friend constituted "plotting," then a conversation in my cabin would likely end up as an early evening quickie.

The man could read minds, because he said,

"How about the conference room at the Writer's Retreat? And we can order some food, because I haven't had a chance to eat and I'm starving."

Fairmont tugged gently on the leash as he stood up and leaned against Luke's leg. Absent-mindedly, Luke reached down and scratched behind my dog's ears.

Fairmont really liked him. Who was I kidding, *I* really liked him. And I hated to see anyone skip meals, myself included, so I agreed. "On one condition. Anything that you know that is also known by the entire town of White Sage, you share with me."

He looked conflicted—likely because Deputy Zapata had a big mouth when it came to his mama —so I crossed my arms and waited. It wasn't an unreasonable request. I just wanted to be on equal footing with the locals, and I might as well do that by getting my information straight from the best source in town.

"Fine." He pulled out his cell phone. "Pizza, Chinese, or sandwiches? Your choice, my treat."

My stomach decided it was a great time to protest the coffee I'd had in lieu of a decent meal, so it looked like this was a win-win. "Does the sandwich shop have soup?"

15

After a quick potty break and doggie snack, I left Fairmont in the stone cottage happily cuddled up in his bed with his favorite stuffed bear.

When I entered the conference room, Luke was just tipping the delivery girl.

"Thanks, Uncle Luke." The teenager pocketed the cash and, with a quick grin in my direction, made a hasty exit.

I looked at him. "Uncle Luke?" If I wasn't already thinking this town was an oddball combination of a small high school and a large family, that confirmed it.

He shrugged and gave me a sheepish look. "Annie works at her mom's shop, and my sister makes the best sandwiches in town."

"Of course she does," I murmured, then took a seat at the conference table.

"Welcome to White Sage, where everyone's related to someone. Speaking of, who are your people in town?" He passed me a container of soup then sat down next to me. "You mentioned a local connection."

"Ah, I wondered when you'd get around to asking that. She wasn't exactly local, more transplanted. My aunt moved out this way after her husband died. Meredith Stoker?" I paused as I unwrapped my sandwich to see if he recognized the name.

"Ah, yes. She was the head librarian at the county library for several years. She passed away about five years ago?"

I nodded.

"That was when I was still living in Austin, so I missed the funeral. I'm sorry for your loss."

"Thank you. I was very fond of her, though I didn't see much of her the last few years of her life. She didn't travel, and I..." And I, wrapped up in my failing marriage, hadn't made time to travel to White Sage. I felt bad about it, even though Meredith would never have expected it. "Well, I just didn't see enough of her before she was gone."

Whether the somber topic killed the conversation or we were both that hungry, we abandoned conversation and tucked into our food.

Once we'd both taken the sharpest edge off our hunger, I said, "So, I was plotting with Helen at The Drip? That makes me sound like an anarchist."

He eyed me over his to-go cup of iced tea. He set it down and said, "Don't even try to deny it. I know Helen Granger. And I'm starting to get some ideas about you." His lips quirked, but his amusement vanished in a flash. "This is a murder investigation. You can't involve yourselves, you can't interfere in our investigation, and you certainly can't do any investigating on your own."

Since that was exactly what we'd planned— albeit more focused on the canine-feline angle than homicide—it was hard to be too terribly upset that he'd suspected us. On the other hand, two women should be able to meet in a public place without concerns of big brother (or a skinny, over-tipped barista boy) watching over our shoulder.

There was something *else* I had every right to be upset about, though. "How is it that everyone knew it was a murder investigation before I did? I'm a witness. Actually, I'm a victim as well, since the crime was perpetrated on my property."

"It wasn't."

"Oh?" I asked casually, then sipped my club soda.

Luke wasn't buying it. Skepticism and amusement combined to produce a mouth-watering smile. "All right. I'll give you a few pieces of information that have likely made their way to the public by now."

I couldn't resist a cheerful grin.

"I'm sure I'm going to regret this." He shook his head. "First, there's no question that it was a murder. The method of death—"

"Garden snippers to the heart."

His eyes narrowed. "Carmen Zapata had a hair appointment today, didn't she?"

I felt just a little bit bad for Deputy Zapata, not that he didn't deserve the talking to I sensed in his near future. But I wasn't about to rat him out. I was no skinny barista boy.

Luke rubbed the side of his neck again. "It appears from evidence at the scene—"

I inhaled, ready to pounce on that evidence, but Luke wasn't going for it.

"No, I'm not sharing the specifics. There was evidence, and that evidence points to the injury taking place in the narrow strip of land between your yard and Sylvester's. After he was injured, Sylvester made his way into your yard and collapsed. It's a miracle he made it the few feet that he did, especially since he went over the fence and not through the gate."

I went through the logistics in my head. My gate

was located on the left side of the house, and Sylvester's home was on the right. No way he climbed the fence, so he must have literally flipped himself over it. It was only four feet high, and actually a little lower on that side because of some uneven ground.

Luke leaned his forearms on the table. "Are you sure you're okay with this? It's not too gruesome for you?"

"You haven't even said the word 'blood.'" I patted his hand. "I'm fine. So, do you have any leads, any suspects?"

He chuckled. "If I hadn't done a background check on you, I'd wonder if you'd been up close and personal with a murder investigation before."

"I'm very vanilla...criminally speaking." I blinked innocent eyes at him. My daughter would die of mortification if she could see me now. "Do you background-check all the ladies, Sheriff McCord?"

He leaned back in his chair, and the amused expression returned. "Just the ones who are intimately involved in murder investigations, Ms. Marek. And I'm not commenting on leads or suspects, because you don't have any use for that information—since you're not doing any investigating." He snapped his fingers. "Oh, and also because there's an ongoing criminal investigation."

I bit my lip.

"No promises not to investigate?" he asked. "Because it would make everyone's life easier, and keep both of you safer, if you'd leave everything to qualified investigators."

I wasn't about to make that particular promise, so I sidestepped instead. "You know about the dog and cat problem in the neighborhood?"

He sighed. "I know that Helen lost her dog, and that he was a terrier and unsupervised in the yard. He could have dug out."

"She says the side gate was wide open."

"Oh?" That had him looking concerned.

"You know about May's dog and the gate, don't you?"

He nodded. "What's this about cats?"

"Helen says she's noticed several signs posted for lost cats crop up just in the last few weeks." I almost told him that we'd agreed she should take pictures of them on her next few walks, but he might consider that "investigating."

"Whether there's a problem with missing pets or not, I don't see the connection to the murder."

Or perhaps he *wouldn't* consider it investigating. Hm.

"Zella, I can see the wheels turning in your head. What's up?"

"It's just that Sylvester was May and Helen's best suspect for the disappearances." I felt a little silly talking about the older women's petnapping investigation. "Maybe there's some kind of connection between the two cases."

It sounded just as far-fetched out loud as it had when Helen proposed it.

And yet—I couldn't believe such a small patch of a neighborhood could be harboring two criminals committing unrelated crimes around the same time. Maybe I needed to look at crime statistics to get a better grip on reality.

"So what you're saying is that May and Helen should be our top suspects." Luke gave me a quizzical look.

"No, of course not." I huffed out an annoyed breath. "You're teasing me, aren't you?"

"A little. May and Helen are the dynamic duo of the neighborhood. They can plan a lot of things—including a mean block party and a lively bridge night—but I think murder is outside their skill set."

"But do you admit that there might, just maybe, be something to the disappearing animals—whether it's related to your investigation or not?"

"I have no idea. But now isn't the best time for you and Helen to be poking around trying to find out more." He looked heavenward. "Thank goodness May is visiting her son in Amarillo."

Since I thought a third member would make our little investigation team that much more effective, I didn't comment on May's absence. "So you're not going to look into the animal angle?"

"I didn't say that. All I can tell you is that we'll be following up on several leads." His expression didn't invite further comment, and after a glance at his phone, he stood up. "I have to run. I've still got several hours of work this evening." He held my gaze for a second before he said, "Thank you for having dinner with me. I needed the break."

"Thank you for treating. The sandwich was excellent and the soup even better. Any idea when I might be able to head home?"

"They should be done late tonight or early tomorrow, but I'll give you a call as soon as you have the all-clear. I'm not sure if they'll be done with the yard and alley by then, but that won't prevent you from moving in." His cell vibrated, but after a glance, he ignored it. "So, if everything you own is in your Grand Cherokee, what are you planning to sleep on when you do move in?"

I opened the door and followed him out to the parking lot where the path split off to my cabin. "I have an excellent air mattress."

And instead of eyeing me like I was a crazy lady, he chuckled. "Of course you do. I'll call you tomorrow." He waved as he turned away, and then immediately placed a call on his cell.

Our new home is small. Only one room, and the bed is much smaller. Soft...but small.

The old house had more space, a bigger bed, and lots of squirrels to hunt, but my lady wasn't happy in the old house. She's not happy now, not like she should be, but I have hope there is better for her. I want her to have the same joy, the same comfort, the same love, that she's brought to me.

Soon.

Ah!" My inelegant bark of surprise was accompanied by a full-body flinch, the kind you make when you've been rudely awakened from a deep sleep.

I wiped nonexistent drool from my face and blinked blearily around the room before I realized my phone was ringing.

Fairmont laughed at me from his bed—at least it felt that way—as I snatched my phone from the nightstand.

"Hello?" I refrained from asking who the bleeping bleep called people at the crack of dawn.

"I'll make a note: you're not a morning person." The tickle of Luke's deep voice in my ear at this ungodly hour scrambled my brain.

I cleared my throat in an attempt to smooth the

edges of my morning voice and sat up in bed. "In my defense, yesterday was uniquely trying and tiring. I take it you *are* a morning person, Sheriff McCord?"

A glance at the digital clock on the stove verified it wasn't nearly as early as I'd thought. Unless I'd turned into the teenage version of my children, in which case nine-thirty in the morning was unforgivably early.

"By necessity, not inclination, and it's Luke." He murmured something unintelligible to someone in the background. It sounded muffled, like he'd covered the phone with his hand. When he returned, he was all business. "So, about your house —you're cleared to return. We've blocked access to the backyard for the time being. It's just a precaution, but you'd be breaking the law if you break the seal on the back door, unlock the side gate, or climb the fence."

"That's a very thorough list."

"What I'm hearing is you saying thank you for getting the house cleared so quickly, and also that you wouldn't think of violating the law, especially in regard to interfering with a murder investigation."

I couldn't contain a smile, and I was sure he heard it in my voice. "I said all that, did I?"

"You did," Luke said firmly. "Are we in agreement?"

I drew a deep breath, wondering if I should

outline some very important exceptions—fire, to name one—when he said my name in a warning tone. I caved. "All right. And if you'd given me a chance to wake up a bit, I promise I would have thanked you for working so hard to get my house cleared."

The sheriff was putting in some serious hours, because it *had* been fast.

"Um-hm. Oh, I left you a little something on the porch. I thought you might like it—or find it useful."

He hung up without giving me an opportunity to decline the gift. Clever guy. I wasn't one to accept presents from men I barely knew.

And there was the small consideration that my ex had a tendency to give me gifts when he'd done something wrong. Expensive, guilt-ridden gifts. I'd sold all of the jewelry and put the resulting funds aside for the children. In the end, at least something good had come from them.

But this was Luke, not my ex-husband. The sheriff deserved to be judged on his own merits and not the actions of a person who'd turned out to be less of a man than the boy I'd married so many years ago. Who would have thought time would make him less mature?

But that was irrelevant. My *ex* was irrelevant.

I corralled my meandering thoughts and focused on the here and now.

A gift. From Luke. We had no history and therefore no basis for guilt. A guilt-free gift. A just-because gift.

A smile crept across my face, and a little bubble of happiness welled in my chest.

I fed Fairmont then checked out of the Hiker quick-ish. I hadn't stocked my tiny kitchen with groceries, because I knew I wouldn't be there long, and the sandwich from my early dinner yesterday wasn't stretching into today.

As we headed back into town, I confessed to Fairmont, "The Drip is calling my name. It's shameful, really. I should boycott that place after they ratted out Helen and me."

Fairmont peered at me curiously, but he didn't lift his head from the seat.

"You're right. I shouldn't let the actions of one skinny, goateed boy ruin a perfectly good coffee shop."

Since Fairmont didn't disagree, I decided to stop by The Drip for a slice of quiche and a hemp milk coffee.

Just my luck. Goatee boy was working. But then I saw the look on his face and decided fortune might be smiling.

He shot me a sheepish look and a blush stole across his face. Before I could order, he said, "Your coffee's on me today, ma'am."

I gave him a polite smile and decided to give him a teeny bit of a hard time. "Oh, why is that?"

His blush spread to the tips of his ears. "I, uh, I might have... Well, you see, my dad called on my break..."

I tipped my head and blinked innocently.

He exhaled. "I told my dad I met the lady who found the dead, uh, Mr. Wofford, you know, Sylvester. And then he quizzed me, and I mentioned you were here with Ms. Helen, and then..." He grimaced. "I didn't think about it until I'd already hung up, but my dad is really good buddies with Sheriff McCord, and everyone knows that Ms. Helen and the sheriff—"

He stopped abruptly.

I waited to see if he'd say what everyone (except me) knew about Helen and the sheriff, but no luck there. I gave up and let him off the hook, both declining his offer to buy my coffee and tipping him.

He was actually quite sweet. And there was a lesson buried in his red-faced apology. Things were not always as they appeared, and context was key.

Before I left The Drip's parking lot, I called Helen to let her know I'd picked up an extra slice of quiche and a few pastries, in case she was peckish, and confirmed that we were still on to meet at my house. We'd made plans to discuss Helen's findings from her evening walk, and she'd also offered to lend her card table and folding chairs until I could find something more permanent.

Her confirmation was eager, which meant she'd found something.

Anticipation or hunger had my stomach doing a nervous dance. Since the scent of cheesy baked eggs now permeated my car and I liked to think I wasn't a nervy, anxious type, I decided it was hunger. Considering the logistics briefly, I opted to eat my quiche one-handed as I drove. There was no traffic and I was starving, but I'd certainly have gotten after my kids if they'd done the same.

Maybe White Sage was more than a new start. Maybe it was the onset of my own personal rebellion.

Crumbs in the car, especially when I had a washable seat cover, might not seem revolutionary, but as I'd just learned, context was key. I'd lived in a "just so" house for over a decade. And with a sporty, pristine vehicle, and expensive clothes, and a workout schedule that had begun to reach obsessive levels over the last few years.

Quiche in itself was a rebellion. Quiche crumbs? Most definitely so.

And on those too-weighty thoughts, I arrived at my new house to find my gift.

My surprisingly *pink* gift.

So pink, I easily spotted it from inside the car as I pulled into my driveway.

A bright pink lounger took up about a third of my small porch.

Luke had taken my comment about developing a secret passion for pink to heart. (And possibly was poking fun at my air mattress sleeping solution.) I left Fairmont in the car while I got a better look and found that a note and a surprisingly heavy small box occupied the seat. I set both aside so I could better admire my pink gift.

It was outrageously tacky, and I loved it.

And a gift, any gift, had to mean I was off the official suspect list. Though I was still a witness, and a county sheriff really should know better. I should probably return it. I grinned—or not. It seemed to rude to send such a thoughtful gift back.

A text from Helen letting me know she'd be here in a half-hour or so reminded me that I had a dog waiting patiently for me and a car to unpack.

After a quick potty in the front yard, Fairmont was eager to get a look at his new home. Or he was until he caught sight of Luke's gift. One good sniff and he hopped right up onto the porch's new, near-neon addition. He curled into a little ball and looked so comfortable that I tied his leash to the porch and left him there.

I needed to unload a few things from the car, and this would keep him safely out of the way while the front door stayed open.

After two trips to grab the essentials, I decided I might as well keep unloading until Helen arrived.

"Hello!" a sturdy, dark-haired woman in her fifties called from the sidewalk. She was dressed in yoga pants and a t-shirt and had comfortable shoes on. There seemed to be lots of walkers in the neighborhood. That boded well, since I'd sold my treadmill and planned to venture out into the wilds of White Sage, neighborhood sidewalks and country roads inclusive, for my exercise.

I waved back at her with a smile, and then gave Fairmont the signal to stay. "I'll be right back," I told him in a firm voice.

He sighed, and I swore for the hundredth time

that he understood me. Shaking my head at my foolishness, I turned to the woman now walking up my drive.

"I saw you unloading your car and thought you might like a hand." She gave me a little friendly wave. "I'm Karen. Karen Bishop, from across the street and over three houses." She pointed to a house that, like mine, was a little on the small side for the neighborhood.

I extended my hand, and she shook it. "Zella Marek. It's very nice to meet you. I appreciate the offer, but there's no need. I can get it." I shrugged. "I have time."

A concerned look crossed Karen's face. "Maybe you shouldn't leave things in your car for too long, since there's been a murder. In your backyard." Her eyes widened when she said "murder."

I wasn't sure what murder and car break-ins had to do with one another, but now I knew why Karen had stopped on her walk this morning. She was looking for gossip, and what could be better than a murder? All right then, if I was getting grilled, she was toting boxes. "You know, you're right. I shouldn't leave these boxes in the car."

Karen proved to be quite strong. She even insisted on carrying the box with the books. We both carried in Fairmont's huge crate. For a dog who could squish himself up into such a small ball, he was awfully tall and leggy. Without a garage or storage shed, I'd have to figure out where to store the thing until I was sure Fairmont wasn't going to need it.

One more trip and that was everything. And all the while, Fairmont didn't stir. I might even have heard a few snuffling snores coming from the pink lounger.

I checked to see that he was still behaving himself and found him belly up, all four feet in the air, and his head thrown back with abandon.

Karen stood next to me with a perplexed look on her face. "That doesn't look very comfortable."

I smiled. "I guess you don't have dogs?"

She shook her head, and a shadow seemed to cross her face. Maybe her pet had been another victim of the supposed dognapper. Seeing her distress, I couldn't bring myself to ask.

"It's a very popular position, I gather." I pulled my cell from my back pocket and snapped a quick picture. I showed Karen the resulting image. "The pink lounger makes the shot, doesn't it?"

She nodded, but again didn't respond and looked tense.

Before I could smooth over any accidental goof I'd made, Helen pulled up to the curb in her tiny red hatchback.

Karen cleared her throat. "You've already met Helen, then." She didn't seem particularly enthused by the fact.

"She's dropping a card table off for me, and we're going to have a bite to eat. We have more than enough pastries, if you're interested." I glanced up from the text I was shooting Luke. Pink lounger with spotted dog relaxing—it was too cute not to send.

"No, I'm off to work now." She perked up. "But if you're looking for someone to do cleaning, that's what I do. I have a small cleaning service. I'll drop a flyer by for you later."

Or I could just look up the website. I hesitated to ask in case she didn't have one. White Sage wasn't Austin, and I wasn't sure that small businesses in town would necessarily have a website. But my neighbor was gone before I could make a decision. She was across the street before Helen had even popped the hatch.

I joined Helen at the back of her car. "I've got pastries waiting."

Helen's gaze was riveted to the porch. "That's not all you've got. Your dog's taken up residence on a fuchsia lounge chair."

"A gift from Luke," I said with a grin. "I didn't realize it until recently, but I'm rather fond of that shade of pink. I might have to invest in a flamingo or two for the front lawn."

Helen chuckled, and I decided I wouldn't tell her I was serious until the pink lounger had grown on her just a tiny bit more.

Doing a quick calculation of weight versus awkwardness, I said, "I'll grab the chairs and you get the table?"

"Sounds good." She stopped to wave as Karen drove by in a large sedan with a magnet on the side that advertised her business.

"She helped me unload, but I'm pretty sure she was here for gossip. Not a day in town and I'm already the lady with the dead guy in her yard." I winced, then looked skyward and said, "Sorry, Sylvester."

With a wry look, Helen said, "I'm not so sure that's where he'd go. Who doesn't like small children and dogs?" Then she toted the table up the path to my front door. She stopped to snigger at Fairmont, who was still belly up and feet in the air. He wasn't asleep, and when he heard Helen's laughter, he leveled her with a baleful look. She smiled and said, "That's right, Fairmont. You tell the naysayers where they can go. Good boy."

A folding chair under each arm, I followed Helen into the house through the living room and into the kitchen. "You're really not surprised that a neighbor offered to help me unload my car just to get some scoop?"

"Not at all. She was just the first. Trust me." She paused in the act of popping the legs out. "I'm surprised she didn't have her grandson with her. Today's a teacher in-service day."

At my inquisitive look, she said, "She's raising him. Her daughter, the little boy's mother, passed on when he was not much more than a toddler, and no one knows where his dad is."

Which made me think of my ex. He *had* stuck around. I had to give him that. And even though we'd split when Greta and Mark were both grown, he'd still worried about how it would affect them.

I could only imagine how terrible it must have been for that little boy to lose the one parent he had. "That poor child."

"More like poor Karen. He's an odd kid. Then again, his mother wasn't exactly a model citizen." She almost said more but stopped herself. Then she stood up and dusted off her hands. "I don't suppose you have a tablecloth packed away in one of those few boxes?" Seeing my bemused look, she said, "Good that I thought to bring one."

Helen fetched a cheery blue and yellow tablecloth from her car while I retrieved first the pastries and quiche, and then Fairmont.

I shut the front door firmly, and then entered the kitchen with Fairmont on my heels.

Helen was holding the small gift box and Luke's

card in her hand. "It looks like the sheriff has been busy."

Maybe this is our true new home?

Not so big as the big house, but not so small as the small house. It's a nice size. A good in-between size.

And even though my lady hadn't been entirely pleased with the man I found here, he's gone now. She lights up when she sees the new house, and I think she smells like hope. Hope or cheesy eggs. They smell a little the same.

I love this home.

There's a comfy dog bed that smells like Luke, and Luke is my second favorite person. He gave me a present! I knew he liked me.

I snatched Luke's card from Helen. "I haven't even read that yet. You're worse than my son, and he's got the patience of a flea."

Helen shook the box and something heavy made a clunk-clunk sound. Fairmont's ears perked up.

"Quit that or I won't tell you what it says." I waved the card enticingly.

Helen dropped the box on the kitchen counter, wiggled her now-empty fingers, and looked at me expectantly.

I skimmed the card and couldn't stop a grin. That man.

"What? What does it say?" She leaned in. "It's smutty, isn't it. I knew the sheriff was sweet on you."

A laugh burbled up from deep inside me. Smutty —where did she get such ideas? And since when did being sweet on someone equate with smut? Those two things seemed incompatible.

"He says that the lounge chair is a backup in case my air mattress doesn't work out, and that if I don't like the other gift, he can get me a different one from his uncle's shop." I didn't roll my eyes, but I very much wanted to. Was everyone in this town related?

"Can I open it, then?" Helen asked.

I nodded and read the postscript. "PS, Don't break the seal on the back door or climb the fence." I glanced at the back door and discovered a large, official-looking sticker placed across the seam of the door. I couldn't open the door without breaking it.

My backyard was still a crime scene. Yes, I'd known that, but a sealed back door made it seem that much more real.

"A lock?" Helen held up a padlock.

"For my gate. I'll bet you Luke's got it padlocked with county equipment for now, hence the comment about not jumping the fence."

Helen sipped her latte, but her eyes were big.

She was dying to say it, so I put her out of her misery. "Okay, maybe—just maybe—Luke McCord is a little sweet on me."

Helen hooted. "I knew it."

I shook my head. "Don't you think he's too young for me?"

"Why would you say that? Cougars are trendy

now. But that's neither here nor there, because Luke McCord is around your age."

Maybe when I was in my late sixties or early seventies like Helen, I'd assume everyone in their forties were all around the same age, too. "I'm sure he's younger, and you know how men are."

Helen dithered momentarily between a bran muffin and a cheese Danish.

Fairmont watched her intently and then planted himself next to the kitchen table. I'd have to get a kitchen throw rug just for him, because we'd had a chat about where one might be in the kitchen when one drooled. The right answer was not very close to me, especially when I was eating.

Not that he drooled very often. It was more the intensity of his longing that was distracting.

The silence finally registered, and I looked up to find Helen watching me. I grabbed the cheese Danish that she'd left behind (in for a dietary penny and all that...).

Her eyes followed me as I prepared to consume a quarter of my daily allocated calories in one pastry.

"What?" I took a bite.

"Your husband left you for a younger woman."

It wasn't a question, but I felt the need to confirm —and to clarify. "I left *him*, but yes, my husband enjoyed the company of younger women. Many younger women. That seems to be the trend. Or it was among my former acquaintanceship." Then I took a second, heartier bite of cheesy Danish, and I enjoyed every one of its fattening calories. I was a woman scorned, sort of. I deserved cheesy Danish.

"Luke's a good man." Then she frowned. "Also, you need new friends."

I *had* moved, so I couldn't argue with her commentary on my need for new friends. I'd recognized that my previous social circle no longer met my emotional needs. Probably never had, if I was honest with myself.

As for Luke... I didn't think pointing out that good men both fooled around with younger women and left their wives for them all the time would be particularly helpful. And I didn't want to imply that I thought Luke fit into that category.

It was an awfully big category, though.

Maybe Luke was different. Or maybe he had a thing for older women, which reminded me... "He's run a background check on me, so he has to know how old I am."

"See, not an issue. Let's see if I can remember how old he is. He went to school with Lauralee's daughter, and she was just a few years old than..." She counted on her fingers. "Should be around forty-two, forty-three."

"And he's never been married?"

Helen shook her head. "And no kids that anyone

knows about." She grinned. "And we'd know. Secrets are just about impossible to keep in White Sage."

Hm. Forty-three-year-old men who'd never been married didn't just all of a sudden settle down. Then again, who said I was looking to settle down? One glance at my bare kitchen was enough to remind me that I had other priorities right now.

"Let's see what you found on your evening walk."

Helen gave me a curious look, as if she wasn't quite sure we should be done with the topic of Luke McCord, but then, with a little sigh, she said, "Right. I've got a map." Which she then pulled out of her purse.

There were seven circles, each with a small number inside. Some of the writing was blue, some red. "You found *seven* missing cats?" That was appalling in a small neighborhood.

"Three yesterday, but two more from earlier walks that I just remembered. I know the families, so I could mark them from memory. The blue are dogs and the red cats. My Ace and May's little dog are the blue marks."

"Could you tell how long they'd been missing?"

"The earliest is about five weeks."

Five weeks, seven missing animals from a neighborhood that covered six streets. My stomach turned.

Fairmont's cold nose nudged my hand, and I fondled his ears.

"I'm sending this to Luke." When I retrieved my phone to take a picture, I saw that he'd replied to my text of Fairmont belly up in the pink lounger.

Glad someone's enjoying it. Stay home, stay safe, and don't go in your yard. Should be cleared this afternoon and released.

I snorted. "We've been instructed to stay home and stay safe." I debated whether to send the picture I'd just taken of the map.

Since I could hardly complain about him doing nothing with information he didn't even have, I sent both the picture and the time frame along with a quick key: red for cats and blue for dogs. Then I quickly snapped a selfie of Helen and I very clearly in the kitchen with the unbroken seal on the door. *See? At home.*

His reply was immediate: *For how long?*

Excellent question. I pocketed my phone without replying. "So, Helen, what are our next steps?"

Helen and I decided that she'd have a look for more posters on her midmorning walk, and she'd try a new route to see if there were signs of petnapping outside of our little neighborhood. There were two equally small neighborhoods that bordered ours, and her new route took her through the near edges of both.

My assignment was to sort through my boxes and get as squared away as a person with no furniture could. And then to go grocery shopping. An investigator with no food in her fridge wouldn't be able to properly focus on her investigation—or so Helen claimed.

Other than making sure I didn't starve, Helen seemed unconcerned about my lack of furniture and supplies. She didn't even pressure me to run out and buy a bed. I could see a bright future for my and Helen's friendship.

Feeling very much the lesser contributor in our partnership, I said, "I'll try to get a look at the crime scene, as well. Get a few pictures, if I can get close enough."

The strip between Sylvester Wofford's yard and mine had been cordoned off, and I didn't know when it would be released.

Helen gathered up the garbage and threw it into a trash bag that I'd hung from my back door. "If you can't, then just wait. Sounds like you're getting your yard back later today, and then you can take pics from behind your fence."

"Will do. Wouldn't want to upset the sheriff."

She pointed a finger at me. "Or make him arrest you. That would be awkward for him, given his current feelings for you."

I smiled and shook my head. She was awfully persistent in her matchmaking.

Which made me wonder if the history that goatee boy from The Drip had been referencing wasn't more to do with Helen's past misdeeds than the sheriff's. Luke had said that she and May could be busybodies.

"Yoo-hoo." Helen waved. "You're looking a little tired. Maybe save the grocery run till after you've had a nap. And you've got that cute little lounger on the porch that you can use."

"I might just do that."

She nodded briskly. "All right, then. Our plan's in place, and now I'm off to do a little work around the house before my walk. I'll call you when I get home with an update."

"Sounds good. And let me know if you think of anything else I can do." A knock at the door startled me, and Fairmont let out a deep woof.

"Looks like you'll be busy fielding questions from neighbors and being welcomed to our little corner of the world." She wrinkled her nose. "No nap after all."

"I guess murder will stir people's curiosity."

"Murder, yes. But also the pretty lady who moved in with a dog and no furniture." Helen leaned in to give me a parting hug.

I chuckled as I patted her on the back. "Thanks for that."

Helen exchanged greetings with my new visitor, whom we'd caught just as she was about to knock a second time. But then Helen slipped by, escaping with a wave, and I was left to chat about murder and no furniture with Natalie from one street over.

At least she'd brought a fantastic-smelling casserole.

N atalie, the bearer of chicken enchiladas with green sauce (not a casserole) and a very warm welcome to White Sage, was quickly replaced by Georgie, who was then joined by Vanessa.

Neither of them could be any less than eighty, and both had arrived by foot. Georgie without aid, and Vanessa with only a cane. White Sage seemed to house its fair share of spry elderly ladies. That, or they were all flocking to my house like homing pigeons.

While Fairmont eyed them curiously from the perimeter of the room, both Georgie and Vanessa made themselves at home in my sparsely furnished kitchen. Georgiana brought a thermos of coffee with the fixings, and Vanessa brought coconut crème pie with plates and forks.

The two elderly ladies had clearly planned a joint offensive. The pie looked homemade, the coffee smelled fabulous, and they'd worn what I'd guess was their Sunday best. (Though they both had on tights and tennis shoes—quite practical for the fall.) They were definitely going for the "sweet little old lady next door" look, including matching silvery buns and readers attached to thin silver chains.

They were masters.

After I declined a slice of pie—a cheese Danish *and* pie? In one morning? Not happening—I quickly accepted a cup of coffee. Not that I needed the caffeine, but it was the neighborly thing to do. They'd gone to the trouble of giving themselves a means to linger and quiz me at length, so the least I could do was play along and drink a little coffee.

"You're settling in?" Georgie asked as she pulled three place settings of mismatched china cups and saucers from the picnic basket she'd brought. She poured heavenly-smelling coffee from a battered thermos into the three cups. "Everyone's been welcoming in the neighborhood?"

"Ah, yes." But I was barely paying attention to her questions. The china settings might not match, but they were all nice pieces. Not the type of thing I would choose to tote around in a ratty picnic basket. "What lovely dishes."

Georgie blushed and waved her liver-spotted hand dismissively. "Oh, these are just odds and ends."

Vanessa laughed as she added her own contribution: paper plates, plastic forks, and colorful, neatly stitched napkins, each different from the other. "Don't let her fool you. Georgie's picnic dishes are better than most folks' special occasional china."

Running a finger along the delicate floral pattern on my saucer, I nodded.

"You're certain?" Vanessa asked, pointing to the coconut crème pie she'd sliced. "And your puppy, maybe he wants a slice?" When I declined again, for myself and Fairmont (who looked quite put out by my rudeness), Vanessa plated two small slices for herself and Georgie.

"Where did you find these?" I asked Georgie, once again tracing the pretty pattern on my saucer.

"Oh, here and there. Local thrift shops, gifts from friends, you know, that sort of thing. But dear, we're not here to talk about china. We want to hear about the dead body." Georgie's faded blue eyes widened with eagerness. The wisps of white hair that had escaped her bun framed her face and made her look like a rabid angel.

"Georgie!" Vanessa tapped her arm.

Georgie covered her mouth. "Oh, I forgot the plan." She leaned forward. "I was supposed to wait longer before I asked." She turned to her cohort and whispered, "You said after pie, and she's not eating pie."

I suppressed the grin I knew would only encourage her naughtiness. She seemed the sort to get a giggle out of ruffling feathers. At least now I knew who the mastermind was.

Turning to Vanessa, I said, "What exactly did you both want to ask me? I can't imagine I know anything that the rest of the town doesn't. White Sage seems to have efficient channels of unofficial communication."

Georgie leaned toward Vanessa. "What does that mean?"

"We gossip a lot," Vanessa explained before taking a bite of pie.

"Ah, yes." Georgie nodded exuberantly. "That's true. So, what do you know? That way we can tell you what's new and what everyone already knows."

"Georgie," Vanessa said. "Give the woman a moment to at least enjoy her coffee."

I hadn't yet tried it, so I added some cream from the small glass jar Vanessa had brought and took a sip. It tasted as good as it smelled. Better, even. "Delicious."

Vanessa patted Georgie's hand. "You make the best coffee in White Sage, Georgie, dear."

Georgie blushed at the praise, but she hadn't forgotten her main goal. Her attention was still riveted on me.

I drank my exceptional coffee, refusing to be rushed into spilling details I wasn't sure I should share.

The ladies polished off their pie, and when it was clear I wasn't going to jump in with any gory specifics, Vanessa said, "You know, Sylvester was a time bomb."

Coffee went down my windpipe, and with a concerned look, Fairmont moved to lie down next to my feet. Once I'd recovered, I said, "I'm sorry, a time bomb?"

Georgie nodded.

"Well, he worked with troubled children," Vanessa said. "It was just a matter of time before something went awry."

Speaking of bombs, how did I navigate through that particular landmine without offending her? A garden snip to the heart wasn't what I'd call "something going awry." And since when did a career in social work come with a death sentence? Or children with unstable family lives inevitably become murderers?

Probably best to go with conservative, so I said, "I'm not sure I know what you mean."

Georgie snorted. "She's just a dramatist."

"Dramatic," Vanessa translated, then turned to Georgie and said, "No, I am not. It's a dangerous job, working with kids who are into drugs and who knows what."

"Pfft." Georgie tucked one of her wild white locks behind her ear. "Those kids are harmless." She pursed her lips, then said, "Mostly harmless, anyway. No, it's the secrets that got him."

Vanessa considered this for several seconds before replying, "Well, yes, there might be some truth in that."

I still had absolutely no idea what they were talking about. "What secrets?"

The two women shared a look, but it was Georgie who replied. "If we knew that, we'd know who did the deed, wouldn't we?" She mimed a stabbing motion. "With the garden shears."

A little old lady with silvery-white hair, a cardigan, reading glasses on a chain, and a love of fine china was making stabbing motions in my kitchen. I would not laugh. I wouldn't.

Once I was certain I would indeed *not* laugh, I considered whether I should correct her. The killer had used small gardening snippers, not shears. But it was probably best not to admit to any specific knowledge. That would likely open up the flood-gates, and the questions wouldn't end.

Vanessa patted Georgie's hand again. "I think Zella means more generally, not the specific secret."

"Oh, well, I guess you might not understand." Georgie shook her head. "Nothing's a secret in a small town."

But I *did* understand that. Very well. After only a day, it was crystal clear. "If nothing is a secret in a small town, then how did Sylvester Wofford have secrets? And what does that have to do with his death?"

Georgie tut-tutted, as if I'd failed to grasp the simplest of simple ideas. "It's impossible to keep *every* secret, especially in a tiny town like White Sage. But what if someone has managed it, at least for a little while? And when everyone knows every-thing about everyone *except* for the one secret, then that secret is viciously guarded." She smiled at me expectantly. "Do you see?"

I thought I might.

Sylvester Wofford, former social worker, knew someone's secret. The wrong someone or the wrong secret. That was what the ladies were trying to say, in a very roundabout way.

And I thought they just might be right.

My lady has friends!

Friends with sweets, and friends with savories.

Only the very best sorts of people share their food, so I'm sure these new friends are the best sort. I especially like the Georgie and the Vanessa friends. They're almost as nice as the Helen friend.

But none compare to Luke. Luke is the best.

With all her new friends, I'm not certain why my lady is so worried. But she is. I can feel it. She worries, and that saddens me.

T he ladies tried to pack up their dishes and whatnot. But I couldn't let Georgie bring her special china home dirty, and I certainly couldn't let her carry that picnic basket alone.

I promised to wash Georgie's dishes and run them by her house in the next few days, so she gave me her address. She looked quite pleased by the future visit. Turned out she lived just a few houses away.

When I tried to do the same with Vanessa's napkins, she snatched them from me, claiming she couldn't leave me responsible for laundry when I hadn't yet purchased a washing machine. And, terrible influence that she was, she insisted on leaving the pie.

Both of the elderly ladies were careful to take their leave of both me and Fairmont, wishing both of us a lovely day. Fairmont seemed impressed by them, but less than pleased to have missed out on the pie. Or maybe that was my imagination working overtime.

The rest of the morning passed in a series of interruptions, though none quite so noteworthy as Georgie and Vanessa's visit. As soon as I'd dug into a task, a stranger would knock on my door bearing an edible gift. I'd been interrupted hanging up my clothes, sorting my toiletries, and unpacking my books onto the built-in shelves.

With thoughts of avoiding nosy neighbors knocking on the door, and perhaps with a twinge of guilt for my earlier Danish, I set off for a walk with Fairmont.

Except the news was out. The new neighbor who'd found the dead body was a late forties fading blonde with a pointer. So after being stopped on my walk for the second time, I beat a hasty retreat.

I was only a few houses from my front door and my new pink lounge chair—for which I was developing an unreasonable affection—when a woman yoo-hooed me. I almost kept walking, but then I recognized the black mailbox with the bright red ladybugs and realized I was in front of the Severs' house. I turned to find Betsy waving at me, and she was child-free.

I knew the look on her face. I'd worn it enough myself when my children had been younger. Betsy Severs was a woman desperate for a little adult conversation.

She'd offered me the use of her bathroom without batting an eyelash. That was a kindness that I could minimally repay with a quick chat. Once I was settled, I'd bring a small gift over to show my appreciation. Maybe a nice bottle of wine.

Fairmont and I detoured up her front path and joined her on the porch. It was larger than mine, to go along with the larger house.

She gestured to the storm door and said, "Naptime."

I nodded. I'd assumed as much, though looking at her frazzled appearance, I couldn't help thinking it was a shame she didn't feel she could take the opportunity for a quick one herself.

"I can hear them through the screen door," she said quickly, shaking her head. "It's not like they're unsupervised."

Since I hadn't hinted that they were or even entertained the thought, I wasn't entirely sure why she was being so defensive. She hadn't been yester-day, nor had she been so on edge or quite so tired-looking.

I tried to reassure her with a smile. "I'm sure they're fine. Thanks again for yesterday morning."

She nodded, but nibbled at her index finger cuticle. I didn't think she realized she was doing it. Something was wrong. She'd been harried by the cleaning lady's scheduling mishap yesterday, but not overtly stressed. Today she looked overwhelmed.

She glanced at Fairmont. "You're both getting settled in? No problems?" Then she winced. "The murder is obviously a problem, with his body in your yard, and..." She stopped and took a breath. "That's not what I meant. I meant with your unpacking."

His body...not *the* body...

I put a hand on her arm. "It's fine. I know what you meant."

When I touched her, it was like a valve released. Her breath whooshed out and a good bit of the tension she'd been holding in her shoulders fell away. She looked across her front lawn, out into the distance, and I let my hand drop.

Eventually, she said, "I knew him. Sylvester Wofford. The dead man in your yard."

It was an odd statement, considering Sylvester lived a few houses away. I assumed, in a neighborhood of this size, that most of the residents knew one another.

But the way she spoke of Sylvester—*his* body

instead of *the* body, her strange admission of knowing him—I couldn't help but think she knew him in a particular way, and I really hoped it wasn't the way I was imagining. I'd had enough infidelity shoved in my nose to last a lifetime. I would happily live in ignorance of any and all of my neighbors' extramarital goings-on.

Unsure if I should (or wanted to) encourage her, I waited for her to decide if she wanted to tell me more.

Her gaze was unfocused—haunted, even. I barely recognized her as the same busy but cheerful woman who'd welcomed me into her home only yesterday.

"I used to drink." She swallowed. "Too much. After Justin, my youngest, we didn't expect... My first two pregnancies were fine, but once Justin was born, I had a hard time...and I drank."

No wine as a thank-you gift, then. And I could have kicked myself for being so flippant, even in my head. Postpartum depression, which was what it sounded like she might have experienced, was nothing to make light of, and certainly nothing to judge—even if it resulted in an affair.

"I'm so sorry." I would have touched her in sympathy again, but she seemed so fragile and lost in faraway thoughts that I decided it was best not to.

Fairmont nudged my hand with his cold nose, and I reached down to pet him.

Several seconds passed in silence. Finally, her gaze sharpened, and she returned to the present. Looking at me, she said, "Thank you. I appreciate it. I'm much better now." She laughed, but it lacked warmth. "*Usually*. Usually, I'm much better."

"If there's anything I can do—"

"No. It's fine. We've learned how to accommodate the occasional low. I have a part-time nanny, and I've taken a few days off work. My husband is also planning to come home early for the next few days."

And yet here she was, confessing her past alcohol abuse to an almost complete stranger.

A genuine smile spread across her face. "They're always into something, busy doing something. The three of them are so much like their daddy, full of energy." A crash sounded from inside the house. "Building blocks. I know the sound." She flinched but then laughed, and I smiled.

Maybe she just needed a sympathetic ear.

"My son was a terror until he turned about eight. Greta, my daughter, was easily swayed to join him in some of his less admirable antics. I remember how exhausted I would get when they were on a tear. So when I tell you that I'd be more than happy to sit your boys so you can have a night out with your husband, I truly mean it."

She wrinkled her nose and tipped her head, clearly torn.

Fairmont pressed his head against her leg, and she reached down to absently rub his neck.

"I'm a little out of practice," I said, "but I can recruit Helen, and we should be able to manage the three of them together."

She grinned, and it looked as if a weight had lifted. "I was thinking a one-to-three ratio might not work out so well, but Helen tips the balance well in your favor."

"You'll call me when you're ready to take me up on it?"

"I will." She gave me a sheepish smile. "I swear I just wanted to give you a proper welcome to the neighborhood, and then... Well, I don't have any excuse, just thank you."

"Not at all."

Another crash sounded—not building blocks this time.

"Ugh." She winced. "I have to run. It looks like naptime is well and truly over."

"Of course." She turned to go, but I called out, "Betsy? When you said you knew Sylvester Wofford, what did you mean?"

Why? Why did I ask? Because I couldn't help myself, that was why. And there was always the chance that my mind leapt to infidelity, affairs, and nookie with young women (there was a significant age difference between Betsy and Sylvester) more because that was *my* history than because it was the actual answer.

Betsy pivoted slowly in the doorway. "Before we moved to this house, back when I was having difficulties, he was my CPS case worker." A look of pain and maybe anger flashed across her face, and then she disappeared inside.

The storm door swung shut with a *thunk*, followed closely by the firm click of the front door latch catching.

CPS.

Child Protective Services.

Oh my.

Not an affair. Not even close.

There was no doubt that Betsy Severs' demeanor —her mental well-being, even—had suffered a blow between my visit yesterday and today.

In that time, she would have discovered the identity of the man I'd announced finding dead in my yard. Of course she would. White Sage and its ridiculous gossip mill worked at ridiculous speed.

Had his death churned up old feelings? Uncovered old wounds?

Fairmont hit the end of his leash as I stopped suddenly in my tracks.

"Oh, Fairmont."

He backed up a few steps, putting slack in the leash, and looked at me curiously.

"What if Betsy isn't upset about discovering Sylvester's identity?"

He sat down, his gaze never leaving my face.

I whispered, so quietly that Fairmont stretched his neck forward as he listened, "What if she killed him?"

Betsy might have had a motive to harm Sylvester.

Fairmont stood up, shook his whole body, then tugged on his leash. When I didn't immediately follow, he looked back at me. I interpreted his actions to mean, "Hurry it up, lady."

Dillydallying in the street wasn't going to provide an answer to the questions Betsy had raised, so I followed Fairmont down her front path toward home.

As I walked past the last few houses, I considered what I'd learned.

I liked Betsy. That wasn't right; I didn't even know her. I *wanted* to like her.

But Betsy Severs had just handed me a solid motive for murder on a silver platter.

My brief visit the previous morning had revealed that it had been just her and the kids the night of the murder. She'd explained that her house was in a state of chaos because her cleaner had rescheduled at the last minute. I got the impression her husband usually worked late, though I'd have to confirm that.

Just her and three small children. How long did it take to slip outside, stab a man in the heart with a set of garden snippers, and then return?

Longer than a trip to the bathroom? I didn't think so.

Long enough that her children would notice? I just couldn't be sure.

Which meant motive and quite possibly opportunity.

My heart broke a little. *Please, please, please, for the sake of those children and Betsy herself, let it not have been Betsy Severs who killed Sylvester.*

24

My quiche and cheese Danish combo breakfast should have kept me going for hours, but that estimate had failed to include various factors, such as moving around boxes, stress, unpacking, stress, meeting the neighbors, and, oh, stress.

I used to be a nervous eater, but I flipped that coping mechanism into nervous exercise around the time I found out my ex was straying. The new me was opting for more of a balanced approach: minimize stress when possible, prioritize good sleep, talk about my problems, and confront the source of my stress directly.

One of the sources of my stress was definitely the dead body in the yard, and I'd been approaching it as a problem to be solved. Check.

Being the neighborhood's new, reluctant source of gossip didn't make my aspiration list, but here I was, answering questions with a welcoming smile on my face. I didn't want my neighbors to hate me, and I planned to live in this house for the foreseeable future. That qualified as confronting the problem directly in my book, so that was a second, prominent checkmark.

But now I was left with an empty stomach and no immediately edible food. The few casseroles I'd racked up so far required a microwave (which I neither owned nor planned to purchase) or a functional oven (my current oven had been disconnected and was awaiting pickup).

Time for the balanced approach to stress management to kick in. A touch of comfort food wouldn't go amiss, at least until I had time to run to the grocery and stock my ancient fridge. After considering my delivery and takeout options—pizza or Sally's Sandwich Shoppe—I landed on Sally's. It was no contest.

Small problem: they didn't actually deliver. Being the county sheriff and the owner's sister certainly had its perks. And I made a note to be especially kind to Luke's niece Annie next time I saw her.

I'd just discovered my luck was running low, and the pizza place that *did* deliver wasn't open for another few hours, when yet another nosy neighbor knocked.

Don't yell at the nice (though nosy) neighbors.

Smile.

I repeated both thoughts a few times before twisting the doorknob.

As I swung the door wide, all I saw was the Sally's Sandwich Shoppe sticker prominently featured on a large white bag, and I about melted. "I might be in love." But then the person to whom the bag was attached chuckled, and I lifted my gaze to find Luke grinning at me.

"We're all fans of the place, though I'm biased, since my favorite sister owns it." Lifting the bag, he said, "Does that mean I've earned entry?"

"Oh, gosh, yes. I even have a table and chairs, so we have a place to eat. But I haven't made it to the grocery yet, so no drinks…"

"Just a second." He handed me the bag and then headed out to his SUV. When he returned, he had two bottles of water.

"You're my hero." When he shrugged, I said, "No, really. I left lunch much too long, and I probably would have strangled the next person to knock on my door. And then you'd have to arrest me. It's really much better this way. Thank you."

He took the plate I offered him and set his

unwrapped sandwich on it. "Haven't your neighbors been bringing food by all morning?"

"I don't have a microwave, and the stove's disconnected. I was planning on replacing it. I suppose I could have tried one of the precooked options, but my taste buds would have rebelled at the chicken enchiladas served cold."

He shook his head and offered me a to-go cup of steaming soup. "You're right. That doesn't sound very appetizing."

"Exactly, and a terrible waste of an excellent dish. Like I said, my hero." I inhaled the spicy scent of the southwest corn chowder he'd brought. "This one's all mine?"

"All yours. I have turkey chili." He pointed a spoon at the second cup. "You know," he said, eyeing my sparse kitchen, "I have a cousin who sells appliances, and I'm sure he can give you a good deal."

With that very first spoonful of silky, creamy chowder, I could feel myself mellowing. So rather than be annoyed that everyone knew everyone in White Sage, and that half the population was related in some convoluted way, this time I decided it was to my advantage and I should appreciate it for the gift that it was.

"That's excellent news, and thank you, yes, I'd love an introduction to your appliance-selling cousin."

"Really?" He looked surprised by my acquiescence, which meant that I needed to make a better effort to hide my annoyance at some of White Sage's small-town quirks.

I was the interloper. I'd chosen to move to this town, knowing exactly how small it was. It was beyond hypocritical to then turn around and judge a place for the very things that drew me here.

"Absolutely. I'm eager to get set up with a proper kitchen, and the old one simply wasn't going to do." I gestured to the sad, old gas stove I was replacing. "I have it on good authority that it doesn't heat evenly."

He nodded in agreement but didn't display the appropriate level of disgust. Clearly the man had low culinary standards if a simultaneously charred and undercooked meal didn't make him cringe.

It appeared Luke McCord wasn't much for cooking. I'd have to remember to send one of the casseroles home with him.

But maybe not the chicken enchiladas with green sauce.

Inspiration struck. I'd have a small slice of the coconut crème pie after lunch and then send the rest home with him. There were so many wins in that decision. I got to enjoy the pie but not overindulge. Luke got a treat, and Vanessa's pie would be appreciated and polished off in record time, I was sure.

"I'm not just here to make use of your dining

facilities." He knocked on the card table with a knuckle. "Excellent though they might be."

"I figured it was my exceptional company."

He grinned. "Always that. But I've also got good news: your backyard is all yours."

Which naturally had me itching to get out there and have a look.

My enthusiasm must have been obvious, because Luke sighed and said, "I'll walk you around the scene when I remove the padlock and perimeter markers. How's that?"

I grinned at him. "That would be great." I might even manage to sneak a few tidbits of information about the case out of him.

But sneaking tidbits of information reminded me that I was carrying my own nugget of knowledge. I'd almost been able to forget about my conversation with Betsy, what with the visiting neighbors and the unpacking and the challenge of feeding myself without benefit of groceries or food delivery.

Should I mention it or not? My chat with Betsy was hardly evidence. At least, I didn't think it was. But I wasn't entirely sure. And then there was my conversation with Georgie and Vanessa, which made what Betsy had told me seem even more important.

Like the map I'd sent to Luke, he could hardly follow up on something he wasn't aware of...which answered the question of my continued silence.

"Luke, I'm sure you've had a chance to look into Sylvester's background." A wary look crossed his face, and I frowned at him. "I'm not trying to pump you for information. I promise."

His skepticism didn't entirely fade, but he replied, "Yes, of course we've done that."

I nodded and considered if I should allude to Sylvester's connection with Betsy or just make sure that they were looking into Sylvester's past cases.

"What have you found?" He gave his turkey chili a wistful look as he pulled out his notebook and pen.

Well, if he was going to be official... "I spoke with Betsy Severs earlier today, and it's not that I think she's done anything, it's just that she mentioned she had a history with Sylvester." I bit my lip. "An unpleasant history."

He jotted a quick note. "Betsy dealt with him in his capacity as a social worker?"

Was "social worker" an umbrella term for Child Protective Services? How specific did I need to be? It wasn't as if Betsy had asked for my silence, not directly, but I felt bad sharing our conversation. It had felt private.

"I'll take your silence as a yes," Luke said, eyeing his chili again.

"I'm sorry. I just feel terrible saying something that might incorrectly point the finger at Betsy. She seems like a kind woman and a devoted mother."

Luke nodded. "She used to have a drinking problem. Don't frown at me. I'm telling you what anyone would, that Betsy Severs used to drink to excess. She never drove or was violent that I know of, but she did drink a lot."

"I just think that a woman who struggles so much after giving birth deserves more than that oversimplification."

"Okay. Maybe her problems were triggered by the birth of her child. Maybe the drinking was related to postpartum depression. But that would be an assumption, since I don't actually have knowledge of a diagnosis. What I do know is that she had a drinking problem and three small children in her care. I also know that she no longer appears to have that problem. And the *only* reason I'm bringing it up is that I suspect it's relevant to this vague conversation we're having. Did her drinking put her crosswise with Sylvester when he was working with Child Protective Services?"

I nodded. "But I don't know any details."

"I'll check it out." He tucked the notepad away and dug into his turkey chili, but then he paused and gave me a small smile. "Thank you."

Luke was no bull in a china shop. I might have known him for less than twenty-four hours, but I felt like I had a good sense of the man. He'd move forward with the information, but I was sure he'd do so with the sensitivity it required.

I turned my attention to Sally's fabulous southwest corn chowder. I needed to curb the hangry, and I couldn't think of a meal better suited for the job. Sally's corn chowder was bliss in a bowl.

25

The corn chowder was flavorful without being too spicy, and my panini had just enough cheese to make me feel decadent but was small enough that I could finish the whole thing.

And since I wasn't overfull and had a big, active day planned, I wasn't going to feel bad about eating a meal that was calorie-packed. Besides, I wasn't calorie-counting any more, just making generally healthful choices...or I would be when my kitchen was up and running.

"Your sister is a genius," I said as I gathered up the trash.

"She also does prepared meals on the side, if you have any interest. Something to do with making full use of her commercial kitchen." Luke shook his head. "The baker who makes Sally's sandwich bread uses the kitchen in the early morning, and she also leases time at night—before she starts the bread—for her cupcake side business. I can't imagine that kitchen sees much downtime, except when they're cleaning." He shook his head.

His sister sounded like a clever lady. "I need to meet Sally."

He nodded, but his attention had strayed to his phone. It looked like Sheriff McCord was back on the job.

I checked the digital readout on the clock. Two o'clock? Where had the time gone? Ah, that's right, it had gone to neighborly visits. Which reminded me that I was owed a call from one particular neighbor. I'd expected to hear from Helen long before now.

"I need to head out. I am in the middle of a murder investigation, in case you hadn't heard." His grin faded. "What's up?"

"Just a second." I grabbed my phone off the kitchen counter, assuming I'd missed her call during one of the gossip sessions at my front door.

But there was nothing. Not a missed call, a voicemail, or a text from Helen. I called her number, and her phone rolled immediately to voicemail.

Fairmont whined and crawled out from under

the card table, where he'd been waiting for crumbs to fall.

"I can't reach Helen."

"And that's a problem why?" Though he didn't look nearly so nonchalant as his words implied.

"Well, for one, she was supposed to call me. But also, you remember that map I sent you?" Fairmont's cold nose nudged my hand. I gave him an absent-minded scratch.

A wary looked crossed Luke's face. "Yes?"

"Helen was trying a new route today to see if there were more posters. That's why I'm expecting a call. She was supposed to check in and give me her results."

"And she was doing this on her midmorning walk?"

I didn't even question how the Sage County sheriff was familiar with my new friend's walking habits. "Yes."

He swore. "You know which way she went?"

The map we'd used to plot her route was on my phone, but I wasn't sure I remembered it exactly. I pulled up the picture I'd taken for Luke and then blew it up as best I could. With a huff of frustration, I retrieved my readers from my purse. With the glasses perched on my nose, I could just make out the street names. A few looked familiar. "Yes. I think so." I looked at the map again and traced the intersecting lines. "No, I'm sure."

"Come on. We'll drive by her house first, just to be sure she hasn't forgotten to charge her phone."

That didn't sound like the Helen I knew, but then again, I'd only met her yesterday. Our instant rapport made it seem longer, but a day was barely any time at all.

Unfortunately, the look on Luke's face didn't reassure me one bit.

Fairmont whined when I grabbed my purse. With all the visitors coming and going, I hadn't had a chance to set up his crate. I didn't think he'd have a problem in the house alone, but I also wasn't sure how long we'd be gone. I really didn't want to abandon him in a new house, for an unknown period of time, amidst unpacked boxes.

"It's fine, Zella. He can ride in the back."

With a sigh of relief, I clipped Fairmont's leash on. "Thank you."

Luke nodded and opened the door for me. The teasing, smiling, flirting Luke was gone, and the man holding the door looked all sheriff.

I tried not to worry. Luke saw the worst of the world in his job, so of course he'd be concerned about Helen's failed check-in. He was intimately acquainted with the terrible things that happened to good people. Just because he was cognizant of and prepared for the worst-case scenario didn't mean it had happened.

My reasoning was sound, but that didn't make the meal we'd just shared sit any more easily in my stomach.

26

H elen had disappeared.

And not by car, since her bright red hatchback was parked in the drive.

Luke knocked on her door, while I held my breath and hoped everything would come up sunshine and smiles.

But no such luck. Helen didn't come to the door, and neither Luke nor I could hear anything from inside.

Luke tried the door and found it locked. He stopped me right as I was about to trample through her beds to check for unlocked windows.

He pointed at a huge flower pot. "Hide-a-key. And as small as White Sage is, Helen has always been diligent about keeping the house locked up, whether she's home or out."

The pot he'd indicated was a monstrous ceramic thing and filled with dirt; it had to weigh a ton. I worked out, and I'd have difficulty lifting it. Helen was fit, but there was no way she could manage it.

"Are you sure? I don't know that I could lift that." I looked closer, hunting for a hidden trick to shifting it. There were large, colorful ants painted all along the outside, each the size of a half-dollar. It was surprisingly whimsical.

"It's not under the pot. It's in it." Luke walked around the pot, his index finger tracing the path of ants until he came to a purple one. He tapped it. "Five legs."

"What?"

He was already poking around in the dirt just above the purple ant. "If you need to break in, for future reference, find the five-legged ant."

He dug around in the pot until he finally pulled out the buried key. It had been nestled under a thick patch of lavender that shared space in the pot with a scraggly bit of rosemary and a much healthier sage plant.

The scent of the disturbed herbs tickled my nose. "Wow. I would have just used a hide-a-key."

"Anything you can buy commercially that's made to stash a key is probably something determined burglars are familiar with. That's what Helen will tell you." He dusted the soil from the key.

"When this turns out to be a misunderstanding, she's going to have my hide for disturbing her plants."

I had no words.

The oddly (and thoroughly) hidden key. The brightly colored, whimsical ant pot. Sage County's handsome sheriff now reeking of lavender. Again, no words.

Not to mention the fact that a law enforcement officer knew how to break into my new friend's home. Why exactly was that?

None of this could be normal, not even in the land of White Sage. It would be comical, minus the fact my new friend was missing. And not *just* missing: missing and last known to be gathering data for a petnapping case that might be tied to a murder.

My pulse pounded as Luke turned the key.

My anxiety probably had something to do with the fact that I was also terrified that something other than the petnapping investigation had befallen Helen, like a heart attack or stroke or... Best not to dwell. Helen wasn't young. It was a simple fact.

"Oh, God, please let her be okay." My breath hitched. I hadn't meant to say that out loud.

Luke lifted his hand and gave me a warning look, and I stopped at the threshold.

"Really?" I crossed my arms, hiding my fear. "You're making me wait? We found the house locked.

In any event, I'll be safer with you than here by myself."

A pained look crossed his face. "This is a terrible idea." He shook his head, but relented and added, "Stay close."

We walked through the house, Luke calling out periodically and me trailing in his wake, terrified we were going to find her unconscious or worse. After traversing the entirety of the house and *not* stumbling upon her body, I realized that my fears might have been exaggerated by recent events.

"Hey, I've got her appointment book here. Give me a minute to call her lunch date." He pulled out his phone and stepped into the next room to make the call.

I took the opportunity to examine Helen's appointment book. It was filled with colorful scribblings. Helen had an active social life, if her day planner was any indication.

Luke returned with a grim look plastered on his face. "She missed a lunch appointment with one of her granddaughters."

Lifting the book in my hand, I said, "Maybe she's visiting with one of her friends and time got away from her."

"Maybe. Let's drive the route. Just in case. If we don't see her, I'll call it in and make it official, but I'm sure we'll find her. She's probably just..." But he came up blank.

Luke thought something bad had happened to her. It was obvious, from the look on his face and the tone of his voice.

He knew Helen better than I did, and while he may have his issues with her (of unknown origin), I knew he liked her. Combine that with his law enforcement background, which included graphic details of the worst acts humans could perpetrate against one another, and I couldn't begin to imagine how he was feeling right now.

After he'd locked the front door, I reached over and squeezed his arm.

He nodded. "I'm sure she's fine." Then he pocketed her spare key and headed briskly for the car.

Once I was settled in the passenger seat of Luke's SUV, I retrieved my readers and pulled up the photo of Helen's route.

Fairmont heaved a sigh from the rear seat as Luke backed out. My dog hadn't even gotten up when we'd gone inside, just waited for us to return, curled up in a tidy ball of fur and floppy ears. Fairmont was handling this crisis much better than I was. My pulse beat fast enough that I could feel the flutter in my neck.

But I had to navigate, so I didn't have time to have a meltdown. With my readers once again perched on my nose, I enlarged the photo of the map on my phone. I called out the name of the street I thought she'd followed, and Luke pulled out of her driveway.

We covered three-quarters of Helen's planned route blanketed in a tense silence broken only by my occasional directions.

I'd been keeping an eye out for any sign of Helen or the posters she'd been hunting and had already spotted one sign for a lost cat. I pointed when I spotted a second lost pet sign attached to a lamppost.

Luke slowed the SUV to a crawl. Only as he pulled to the curb did I see why he'd stopped. Just past the lamppost with the sign was a child's bicycle.

Not so very strange—except there was no child hovering near it.

Worse yet, the kickstand had been ignored and the bike thrown haphazardly next to the sidewalk.

The picture was off. And when you were looking for a woman who might be missing, anything out of the ordinary assumed greater significance. At least, that was how I felt, as I examined the newish bike lying in the grass.

It seemed I wasn't far off the mark, because Luke's features were pinched and tight. He cracked the windows and said, "Stay in the car."

I nodded my agreement. As soon as he closed the driver's door, Fairmont got up and started to whine.

"Take it easy, buddy."

But he wouldn't. He practically vibrated in the back seat.

He pressed his nose against the crack in the rear passenger-side window, whined, then crawled over my seat back, only to shove his nose in the crack of *my* window. He alternated between huffing huge breaths of air and whining frantically.

I hadn't a clue what to do. Telling him to hush wasn't working, and he was working himself into an even more agitated state.

When he started to dig and scratch at the window and door in the back seat, I gave up. This wasn't even Luke's SUV. It was a county vehicle.

"Can't you wait five minutes?" I snapped. I'd never yelled at Fairmont. Not once in the two months we'd been together. But he had to pick now to have a meltdown? When I was out of my mind with worry?

I took a breath, plugged my ears, and tried to think like a not-freaking-out, somewhat rational person. And that was when I realized my poor dog probably had to use the bathroom.

My dog had to pee, and I really didn't want to go to jail because I was responsible for damaging an official county vehicle. Profane words danced in my head.

And as those profane words started to slip past my lips, I decided I had to at least try to keep a handle on my misbehaving mutt.

I hopped out of the car, planning to join Fairmont in the back seat. At least if I was sitting in the back seat, I could keep him from scratching at the SUV's interior. I'd also be able to more closely watch Luke if I could keep a hand on Fairmont's collar. So far, he'd checked out the bike and sidewalk and then made a call.

In retrospect, splitting my attention hadn't been the wisest choice. I had one eye on Fairmont and the other on Luke when I opened the back door...which made me just distracted enough.

My normally mild-mannered dog didn't hesitate when he saw his chance.

He shoved his nose between me and the door-frame, then darted out of the SUV like his rear was on fire.

I love my lady. Desperately. Deeply.
   But sometimes she is just a little bit...dense.

I swore a blue streak, snagged Fairmont's leash from the back seat, then ran after him.

Fairmont and I were in so much trouble.

Luke had said one thing: stay in the car.

Fairmont's initial sprint stuttered to a raucous halt as he barked at something on the ground. He backed up a few feet, looked at me, then charged at the same bug, twig, or speck of dirt that only he could see. And barked. Really barked. Barked like a maniac.

He was so loud that I could barely think—which had my brain drawing parallels I didn't like.

A nasty chill went up my spine as déjà vu hit me. It was the body in the yard all over again.

Except there was no body.

"Oh, God. Helen." The words slipped from my

lips. Because that was who we were looking for—right? That was who was missing. And now...

But there wasn't a body. I scanned the area, double-checking that there wasn't a body. There couldn't be a body. There couldn't be. I'd just met Helen, but I really, really liked her. My eyes agreed: there was no body. But I couldn't shake the similarity between this moment and that of finding Sylvester Wofford's corpse.

And while I had the closest thing to a panic attack I'd ever experienced, Fairmont kept barking. At some bit of nothing.

Clarity hit like a bucket of cold water. That little bit of nothing that had Fairmont hollering so loud his bark was getting hoarse—that wasn't a body. Also, I'd temporarily lost my mind, and now was simply *not* the time.

I'd frozen like a statue several feet away, but my freshly reacquired sense of sanity propelled me forward. I hollered over Fairmont's nonsensical bellowing, "I'm so sorry, Luke."

Luke held out his hand for the leash as I approached, but he didn't look at me. "It's fine. Hold on." He snapped the leash to Fairmont's collar, and the barking stopped.

I leaned down to see what kind of frightening stick or scary bit of fluff had set him off. I leaned closer, and my stomach roiled. "Oh, no. No. Luke, is that blood?"

Luke held Fairmont's collar and rubbed the dog's ears as he nodded. Luke still hadn't looked at me, which was making me even more nervous. Luke pulled Fairmont and me back to the curb and called in his location and other details to his dispatcher.

While we waited for backup, Luke watched Fairmont, and I watched them both. It was as if that smear of blood held Fairmont enchanted. His nose pointed a direct line to it and didn't waver.

Not two minutes later, Deputy Zapata pulled up in a county cruiser. Luke spoke with him, and then they both returned to the spot where I'd remained with Fairmont. Deputy Zapata looked very concerned, possibly scared.

Luke took Fairmont's leash from me. "Dave is going to make sure you're safe. He's going to stick to your side like glue. And you're going to do the same."

I nodded, though I hadn't a clue what was happening.

"You just adopted him, right? From a shelter or someplace that didn't have a history on him?"

"Ah, Fairmont? Yes, about two months ago from the shelter. He was a stray." I frowned and shook my head. "I mean, when they found him. Obviously, he wasn't always a stray." Why any of that mattered right now, I really didn't understand. "What I mean is that he came house-trained and walks well on a leash. That kind of thing. Why are you asking?"

"We're going to see if Fairmont has a natural inclination or if you stumbled on a trained dog at the shelter." I must have looked as confused as I felt, because Luke said, "We're looking for blood, and your dog seems to know blood."

Fairmont had been more alert, more energized in the last half-hour than I'd ever seen him before— except when he'd found Sylvester.

Even now, as we talked and planned, all of his attention was focused on that smear of blood. I covered my mouth with the back of my hand. Maybe Helen's blood.

"You're coming," Luke said, "because if this is a coincidence and he's not actually trained, I don't think he's leaving without you. That dog is usually stuck to you like Super Glue. Are you doing okay? Do you think you can manage that?"

I nodded. Except I wasn't sure what exactly I was agreeing to and wasn't at all sure I wanted to go. If we were looking for blood or a trail of blood, then there might be something at the end of the trail that I didn't want to see.

Luke looked at me, and I could see the concern radiating off him. He was deeply concerned for Helen, so I nodded again, this time more firmly.

Another county car pulled up, except the newly

arrived deputy stayed in his vehicle. Securing the scene? Waiting for more deputies?

"Ready?"

I jerked my attention back to Luke and nodded. When he gave me a hard look, I cleared my throat and said, "Yes. And I'm sticking like glue to Deputy Zapata."

Luke gave Fairmont some slack in his leash, and my couch-potato pooch headed straight for the smear of blood and barked at it again. Luke praised him and encouraged him to keep looking.

I thought my heart might stop, because my spotted, stubby-tailed dog assumed a very businesslike demeanor and did exactly as he was told. He began to sniff: the air, the ground, the grass—everything.

Fairmont explored the surrounding area for what had to be less than a minute or two, then his demeanor changed. Suddenly, he bubbled with excitement and took off down the sidewalk.

L uke is my second favorite human.
Luke is clever.

Fairmont was on a mission. A mission to find Helen's blood. That chill I'd experienced earlier was becoming more persistent. I rubbed my arms.

Deputy Zapata must have taken Luke's instructions to heart, because right away he asked if I'd like his jacket. He really was keeping a close eye on me.

I declined. But I also decided I needed to put my big-girl panties on. This wasn't just Fairmont hunting for blood. This was us, all of us, hunting for Helen.

And we'd find her.

We would.

A round of barking, the third now, interrupted my sensible pep talk. The sound scrambled my brain. Which was part of my problem. Every time I'd convince myself that Helen was fine, that we were just about to find her, that we'd all laugh over the misunderstanding, as soon as I'd lulled my fears, Fairmont would let loose with those brain-jangling barks.

Thank goodness Luke didn't have a problem keeping his head around the noise. It didn't seem to faze him at all. With each round of barking, he encouraged Fairmont to keep looking. Bless my darling dog, but he did. Every time.

It was becoming increasingly clear with each round of barking, each movement forward on what I'd begun to realize was a blood trail, that Fairmont had been hiding some unusual talents. If only he could talk.

What had he done the first five or so years of his life? Maybe there was a way to find out. If he really was trained, there couldn't be that many dogs like him in the area. I made a promise to myself that I'd look—once we found Helen safe and whole and had put this whole day behind us.

We'd already passed two houses following the sidewalk, hopped up into a yard, hung out there long enough for me to notice that the second deputy was following us in his cruiser, and finally returned to the sidewalk.

When we started up into the yard of another house, Luke held up a hand, stopping us. He joined us on the sidewalk. Handing me Fairmont's leash, he said, "You two are waiting in the car."

"I don't understand. What's happening?"

Luke shook his head as he handed me off once again to Deputy Zapata.

As Dave ushered Fairmont and me into the back seat of the cruiser, Luke spoke through the cruiser's window with the deputy behind the wheel.

The deputy confirmed that he'd reached the owner at his place of business, and Luke had his permission to be on the property and enter the home if necessary.

Leaning forward, I asked, "Do you know where Helen is? Or what's happened to her?" But I realized belatedly Luke was still speaking to the driver, he'd just lowered his voice. I put my arm around Fairmont as I waited.

He was sitting in the seat, ears alert. He watched the world through the front windshield with keen interest, but he'd dialed back on the vibrating energy he'd shown earlier.

Luke continued speaking to the deputy in low tones, his body tilted so his back was to me. I couldn't pick up anything he was saying, and it was ratcheting my anxiety up to terrifying levels.

She'd just been looking at lost-and-found posters.

Yes, we'd both thought there was some connection between the pets' disappearances and the murder, but that was due to proximity. And hope. Hope that our little neighborhood wasn't hiding criminals around every corner.

I glanced at the house whose curb we'd commandeered. I let my earlier hope extend and hoped that this tidy house, with its manicured lawn and dark pink, not-quite-red door, wasn't hiding a criminal—or something worse.

Finally, Luke turned his attention to me. "I can't explain now, but I recognized the bike and I know who works here."

Then he was gone, taking Deputy Zapata with him.

Luke had recognized the bike. The child's bike. I'd forgotten about it completely.

It was a teacher in-service day, so that shouldn't be so very strange, should it? If kids weren't in school, then they rode their bikes around the neighborhood. And children weren't always responsible with their possessions, even favored items like bicycles.

Kids. Bikes. Neighborhoods. The three tumbled around in my head, trying to connect. A soft sigh made the lips around Fairmont's muzzle puff out for a second. Which then had four words tumbling around in my head: kids, bikes, neighborhoods, and dogs.

An image of the missing-pets map popped into my head. All of the animals were missing from an area that was walkable, but only be a very energetic, fit, determined walker. A bike, on the other hand, would make quick work of the area.

Even a child's bike.

No.

That couldn't be.

A soft sound of protest made me realize that I was clutching Fairmont quite tightly. I rubbed him apologetically and turned my mind away from the disturbing thought of a child being involved with the pet disappearances.

Something else Luke had said nibbled at the back of my brain. Something about knowing who worked inside the house.

A residential home with owners who had to be telephoned at work for permission to enter—so they weren't working from home.

Who worked at the house? I was sure Luke knew just about everyone in White Sage, so that wasn't helpful. But the type of work might certainly narrow it down. Plumber, gardener, cleaner...

Oh, Lord, was I slow. It was the woman with the cleaning service. The woman who was raising her daughter's ten-year-old child. Karen, that was her name.

But just because Karen worked in the home

where the blood trail had ended didn't mean that she was tied to Sylvester's murder or that she'd had harmed Helen in any way.

Except reality was knocking, and I couldn't deny any longer that the blood Fairmont had found was most likely Helen's. Helen, who had walked that very route not so long ago. Helen, who had missed lunch with her granddaughter. Helen, who was almost definitely missing.

I shook my head. Maybe the killer and the petnapper were two different people—they were two very different crimes—but the violent act near the child's abandoned bike exactly on the route that Helen had taken, a route that led to even more missing pet posters, made me doubt two separate criminals were involved.

And if there weren't two people committing all of the crimes, then whoever had hurt Helen had likely also killed Sylvester.

Both crimes of opportunity, Helen in the street on her walk and Sylvester as he'd been gardening. He was an avid gardener and had been killed with his own garden snippers. Was it such a stretch?

But then the pets... The pets had to be tied in as well somehow.

So many of the pieces were weaving together, but not the pets.

Betsy! I'd forgotten all about her. If Karen was

the murderer, then Betsy Severs, recovering alco-
holic and mother of three little boys, had nothing to
do with Sylvester's murder.

"Oh my. Betsy—her cleaning lady cancelled last
minute." And if Karen was her cleaning lady...
"Oh my."

"I'm sorry, ma'am?" The deputy turned in his
seat.

But I just shook my head. I couldn't get all of my
bouncing thoughts and scattered theories out in a
coherent manner, and I wasn't even going to try.

Fairmont nosed me.

I'd squeezed him too hard again. I unwrapped
my arm from around his shoulders. No reason for
him to suffer excessively tight hugs just because I
was distressed.

I clenched my hands, as a pulse of guilt so strong
it made my insides shudder hit me.

Betsy had given me a clue, but I'd failed to see it
amidst the noisy details of my life. The past two days
had been crammed: the investigation, my new
friendship with Helen and quite possibly Georgie
and Vanessa, my attraction to Luke, and settling into
the house.

With all of that, one simple but very important
fact had slipped past my notice.

The morning I found Sylvester, Betsy had told
me about her cleaning lady cancelling. The change

in routine had thrown her household into an uproar, especially with the unwashed laundry she'd been catching up on. Evidence of the cleaning lady's absence had been literally piled up around me.

I'd thought Betsy had the opportunity to kill Sylvester, because neither her cleaner nor her husband were home. Why hadn't it occurred to me that the cleaner had cancelled for a nefarious reason? Or minimally, that the timing of the woman's cancellation was odd.

Guilt at my inability to see such a critical piece of the greater puzzle—and the possible horrifying consequences of that failure—made my stomach roil.

How had I been so blind?

He'll be fine," the deputy said from the front seat.

"What?" I didn't mean to be rude, but what the hell was he talking about?

"Sheriff McCord. He'll be fine. He has a lot of experience with this sort of thing. He was a big-city cop before he came back home."

I hadn't known that, though I had known he'd lived in Austin for a while. I also hadn't been worried about Luke. I'd been far too distracted by guilt and regret to be worried that Luke was in danger. But because of the deputy's ill-timed comment, *now* I was terrified for both Luke and Helen.

Trying to keep the sarcasm out of my voice, I thanked the deputy.

"Everyone knows he's sweet on you." The deputy

looked at me expectantly, like I might open up to him and tell him that yes, Luke and I had fallen for each other on first sight.

Good grief, what was with this town?

My new friend was hurt, maybe worse, Luke might be headed into trouble—and this guy wanted to chat about a possible romance between his boss and me?

Then it occurred to me: if he felt comfortable pumping me for information, then certainly there was nothing wrong with me doing the same.

I glanced at the house. It was still eerily quiet and dark inside. Luke and Deputy Zapata had gone around the back. "Whose house is this?" I read aloud the name tag on his shirt: "Deputy Francetti."

"This is Richard and May Sloan's place. I'd have thought you'd known that, being such good friends with Helen."

We'd known each other for *two* days. Barely. But I swallowed my annoyance with both Deputy Francetti and White Sage's bullet train of gossip. "Oh, yes, of course. And Karen's their cleaning lady, right?"

Deputy Francetti nodded absently. The unintelligible announcements coming through his radio held most of his attention. Then his cell phone rang.

"Sheriff? Yessir. Right away, sir." And he started the car.

"Luke's okay?" When Deputy Francetti nodded, but didn't elaborate, I asked, "Where are we going?"

If we were headed home—

"Round back. I'm supposed to deliver you and the dog." He briefly met my gaze in the rearview mirror. "That's all I know."

Me and the dog? What in the world could they need us for? But I wasn't about to say no. If Luke thought Fairmont and I could help, I was all in. I wasn't even scared, not for myself. Luke wouldn't ask me to do anything dangerous. But I wasn't feeling confident of my ability to participate without making things worse.

It took me a moment to realize we hadn't moved. The deputy waited patiently for my agreement, while I dithered over the whys and the hows.

"Yes. Sorry, yes. Let's go."

From the street, our view of Luke and Deputy Zapata had been blocked by the house. The drive curved around the side of the house and toward the back. But as we rolled up the drive, I got a look. Most notable was Helen's absence.

Deputy Francetti exited the cruiser, shrugged out of his windbreaker, handed it to me, then firmly shut the door with Fairmont and me still inside.

After I wrapped myself in the offered jacket, I allowed myself to take in my surroundings.

A ruddy-faced, angry Karen was cuffed and

being detained by a surprisingly proficient-looking Deputy Zapata. Luke was a few feet away addressing Karen. She didn't reply verbally, only shaking her head. And Deputy Francetti stood guard beside the car Fairmont and I still occupied.

Luke talked to Karen for a few more seconds, then turned on his heel and headed our way. He opened the back door of the cruiser and leaned down to talk to me. "Can you turn Fairmont loose?"

I tightened my grip on Fairmont's collar, then looked around. The street was deserted. "Yes."

"He'll come back when you call him?"

Fairmont had been terribly excited about the dead body and he'd still come right back when I'd called him then, so I couldn't imagine he wouldn't here. I nodded. "Why?"

Luke squinted at me. "We haven't found Helen. I want to bust open the trunk, but... It's complicated. No warrant. I shouldn't need one, but—"

"Yeah, that thing in North Sage Grove." Deputy Francetti nodded like it all made sense.

Luke blushed and frowned at Francetti. "Anyway, turn him loose when I tell you to, all right?"

"Okay, I've got it." I waved him away. Whatever was going on, there was an urgency to the situation, and we didn't need to sit here and debate. I kept a firm hold on Fairmont's collar as Luke returned to where Deputy Zapata was detaining Karen.

He left the cruiser door open, which gave me an excellent view but no sound. They were too far away for more than the subdued murmur of voices. I waited for his signal and hoped that Fairmont was supposed to be hunting for blood traces and nothing else.

Something Luke said to Karen made all her color wash away. She swayed with obvious distress but didn't speak. She shook her head once, nothing more.

"Go ahead, Zella," Luke called. "Let the dog hunt."

Fairmont had been zeroed in on Karen's sedan for I didn't know how long. I hadn't noticed until I went to turn him loose. As I unhooked his leash, two things happened.

Karen screamed obscenities at me and crumpled to the ground hollering all sorts of nonsense that I couldn't begin to understand.

And Fairmont ran straight for the tail end of the car. He started barking at it before he even reached the trunk. He backed up, looked at me, and then barked at the trunk again. He circled around to the side, came back to the trunk, and barked some more.

Not like the blood drops he'd found.

Just like the corpse he'd discovered.

She was dead inside that trunk. Lovely Helen, grandmother to I didn't even know how many grandchildren and my new friend, was dead. I sank to the ground, my knees no longer able to support me.

Francetti appeared with a crowbar and pried the trunk open. Luke grabbed hold of Fairmont and pulled him away. And all the while, Karen screamed and sobbed, and I stared.

Sounds faded to a muted hush and the end of my vision narrowed. Shock, probably. Because Helen was gone.

I could see on their faces that they'd found her. The shock, the disgust, the anger—it was all there.

A few seconds and an eternity passed, then Luke called out, "She's alive!"

Several seconds passed before I understood his words. Alive. She was alive. Helen was alive.

If I hadn't already been on the ground, I would have keeled right over from relief.

Thank the heavens and Fairmont and Luke and Deputy Zapata. I could kiss them all.

But then I had to expand my thanks, because the paramedics arrived. And then there was a nice deputy who held Fairmont's leash, and the nice paramedic who was offering me oxygen.

"No, I'm fine. Thank you."

The woman leaned down closer to me. "You're not fine. Take the oxygen. It'll help."

I motioned to Helen, who was being pulled from the trunk. She looked so tiny, and there was blood—

The paramedic moved to block my view. "There's a team working with her. You need to think about you right now.

"My dog—"

"Is being looked after. The sheriff made sure of it." She grinned. "Everyone says he's sweet on you."

I laughed hysterically. "That's what I hear. Give me that oxygen."

I like Helen. Not as much as Luke, but a lot. She gives good scratches and smells like kindness.

I'm sad she's hurt, but I worry more for my lady. Her tender heart breaks over the hurts of her friend.

Once my shock had been alleviated by oxygen, a warm blanket, and a little time, I started to read between the lines. No one would come right out and say that Helen was fine. Which meant that she either wasn't or they weren't sure yet.

So when Lisa the paramedic said I was cleared to go, and Deputy Francetti said he was to drive me and Fairmont home, I said quite firmly, "No, thank you. I'd like to go to the hospital where they've taken Helen."

Deputy Francetti looked at Fairmont, who'd made his way to me during all the hubbub, dragging the very nice, leash-holding deputy with him.

Fairmont's designated leash-holder had relinquished him to me when my spotted pal had wedged himself half on top of me. Twenty minutes later, his shoulders and head were still on my lap.

"It's one town over in North Sage Grove, and the dog can't go inside with you." Giving me a sympathetic look, Francetti said, "I get it. We're all worried about Helen. But her family is going to be there when she wakes up, and you guys look beat. Besides, you were both there when she *really* needed you. Right, buddy?" He petted Fairmont's head.

I weighed the options and decided that napping first might be wise. It didn't hurt that Deputy Francetti sounded confident that Helen *would* wake up. I could always put the hospital on speed dial and check on her by phone. "You're right. Of course you're right. Thank you, Deputy Francetti. You've been very kind."

"I'd like to see what the sheriff did if I wasn't." He winked at me.

At least he didn't comment again that Luke was sweet on me. If I heard that one more time, I refused to be held accountable for my actions.

A KNOCK at my door woke me. I'd been sleeping so hard that the sound jerked me awake, and I fell out of bed.

Thankfully, it was only twelve or fourteen

inches. I rubbed my hip, then patted my air mattress affectionately. It really was quite a nice air mattress.

Fairmont lay spread-eagle, legs pointed skyward, in the exact center of the bed. My bed-hog dog was the reason I'd been huddled near the edge of the mattress, and also why I'd landed in an undignified heap on the floor.

He grinned at me with a look of amusement.

"I'm glad you're entertained."

Someone's fist pounding on my front door reminded me that I hadn't woken on my own.

With a glance at the clock, I saw that it was six-thirty. In the morning.

I couldn't remember the last time that I'd woken that early. Probably not since Greta and Mark lived at home. Dealing with unruly teenagers in the morning required a minimum of two cups of coffee, which required earlier hours than I'd liked. I wouldn't say I was a night owl, but *six-thirty*...

And that was when I realized my level of exhaustion. That moment of blissful ignorance that occurred right after waking and before the reality of the day settled itself firmly in my head—usually only three, four, maybe five seconds at most—had lasted minutes.

The events of the previous evening came back in a rush, and I leapt to my feet. Where was my phone?

After grabbing my phone, my robe, and a frantic breath, I rushed to the door.

I looked through my peephole and saw Luke there, decked out in his official duds. He must have heard my less-than-stealthy approach, because he lifted a to-go cup of coffee and a pastry bag.

"Just a second." I tied my robe firmly around my waist and dropped my phone into one of the over-sized pockets.

When I opened the door, he said, "I did call first." He looked me up and down. "A few times."

Digging my phone from my pocket, I saw three missed calls. "Helen?"

"Awake and asking about you and Fairmont."

A rush of relief made me wobbly.

Luke reached out to steady me. "Hey now. That's good news. She's doing really well. Karen..." He looked at me as if unsure I was up to the news.

"Go on. I'm not going to faint from shock. I promise." I plucked the cup from his hand. "And I'm shortly to be well fortified with caffeine." I waved him inside.

"I was going to say that Karen only managed one blow." He stepped into my living room and shut the front door behind him. "Her grandson Tim saw her hit Helen with a brick and cried out, then he got scared and ran away. Karen stashed Helen where she thought she'd be safe so she could look for Tim."

"Oh, that's terrible. That poor little boy." And I meant it, even though I'd already had the terrible thought that he might be connected to the missing pets. And then I realized the implication of Luke's statement. "If Tim hadn't interrupted her, then..." I couldn't say it aloud. I wrapped both my hands around the warm cup of coffee.

"That's right. She might not have stopped with the single blow to the head. We can't be sure. All we do know is that the trunk was an attempt to temporarily secure Helen, just until she could find the boy. We interrupted her shortly after she'd returned. She had no comment when asked what she planned to do with Helen."

I shivered and sipped at the coffee. It warmed me from the inside out and gave me a stout kick in the pants. Fortified, I asked, "And the little boy—Tim?"

"He's safe. He hid for a while, but he finally went home when he got hungry. That's where we found him. He confirmed that his grandmother struck Helen with a brick."

"Right." My heart hurt for that child. His father gone, his mother dead, only his gran to raise him— and now she was gone, too.

"Helen has to stay in the hospital another night or two until some final test results are in, but she really is doing very well. Truly, she is."

"I believe you. I was actually thinking about the

child, about Tim." I gave my head a small shake. "Tell me more about Helen. How is she feeling? And have you already interviewed her?"

"I did interview her. She was coherent, but in some pain. I'm running over to talk to her again, now that she's had a night's rest. That's why I'm here so early. I thought you'd like to hitch a ride and see for yourself how she's doing, especially since she was asking after you." He looked at me uncertainly, and I didn't want to imagine what I looked like right now.

"A little more coffee, and I'll look human, I promise." I smoothed my tangled hair back from my face. I probably had sheet marks on my cheek. I indicated my disheveled state and said, "But if you show up on my doorstep unexpectedly, this is the risk you take."

He grinned. "I don't even know what you mean. But if you need a little time to, ah—" Wisely, he didn't finish that thought. "What I mean to say is, are you sure you want to ride with me? What with all the calls you made to the hospital, I thought—"

"Yes! I'm sorry. Yes. Yes, I do." I rubbed my eyes. "If I hadn't been so exhausted after everything, I probably wouldn't have slept so hard and missed your calls." I shook my head. "Three calls—wow, I must have been sleeping hard."

As we'd chatted, I'd made a pretty good dent in my coffee. I was almost starting to see the edge of reason. Once I finished the cup, I might even be completely coherent. I snapped my fingers. "Fair-mont. Can you take him out back for a bathroom break? Or walk him? Since you left yesterday before removing the padlocks and the seal, I didn't feel right going in the yard. That seal looks awfully official, and a sheriff warned me not to break it."

"I did say that, didn't I? I'll fetch the padlock and take as much of that tape off your door as I can while you get ready. It slipped my mind, or I'd have sent someone over to handle it yesterday."

Fairmont sauntered in belatedly. He took a moment for a leisurely stretch then trotted up to Luke with his stubby tail wagging.

"It's bizarre how much he likes you. I get it, dogs like you, but he usually is much more reserved with strangers."

Luke knelt down and rubbed his ears. "I bet it's the uniform."

"You weren't wearing one when he first met you, but I don't see why that would help."

"Well, I'm pretty certain he was a search dog before he landed with you, so he might have spent some time around people in uniforms." He shrugged. "Just a thought." He pulled a pocketknife from his trouser pocket. "Go on. I'll take care of the door, the gate, and Fairmont."

I nodded and disappeared into the bathroom.

"By the way," Luke called through the door.

"Before I forget, you sent the night nurses a nice little bouquet for their patience."

I poked my head out of the bathroom. "Rats. Were they ready to kill me? Never mind, I don't want to know, but thank you. I appreciate you thinking of it, and I'll pay you back."

He shrugged.

Maybe calling every quarter hour had been a *little* extreme.

I ducked back into the bathroom and ran the shower. I had time, given Luke's to-do list. I sighed. He really was a good guy, and if I was looking for a keeper, he'd sure as heck be one.

34

L uke spent most of the trip to the hospital on the phone with an old college friend of his on the East Coast. He apologized before taking the call, and then explained that they'd had a hard time catching each other on the phone over the last week and still had some details related to an upcoming trip to sort out. From the sound of it, there was a bachelor party in the offing.

I was happy to have most of the fifteen-minute drive to clear my head and wake up, and even more so when he stopped at a drive-through to grab me a second cup of coffee.

The man was on the phone and driving, and he'd still noticed that I'd drained my cup.

By the time Luke had finished his call, I was mostly awake and we were almost to the hospital.

Grilling him now seemed inconsiderate, since he'd likely have to repeat everything he told me. I didn't get the impression that he'd given Helen an update yesterday, just gathered the bare facts.

So I practiced a little patience and went for small talk. "Thanks for helping me set up Fairmont's crate."

"No problem at all. I hope he got something special last night. That dog deserves a steak after what he did."

A sliver of doubt had entered my mind, and I couldn't shake it. "Do you think someone's looking for him?"

Luke glanced at me with sympathy in his eyes. "I don't know. I can tell you it takes more hours than you might imagine to produce a reliable cadaver dog."

I closed my eyes. Fairmont had found a body, blood smears, and a bleeding person—did that count as a reliable cadaver dog? I always thought they found buried bones and skeletons in walls.

I opened my eyes when I felt Luke squeeze my shoulder.

"What do I know? Don't borrow trouble. And didn't you adopt him from the shelter? If someone were looking for him, that's the first place they'd have looked." He pulled into a parking spot then shut the engine off. "You ready?"

Not at all.

Except he didn't mean finding Fairmont's former owner. And now that I knew Helen was on the mend, I couldn't help but do what Luke had warned me against: borrowing trouble.

What were the chances a highly trained dog, possessing a very specialized skill, had been intentionally sent to the shelter? He didn't *seem* like a washout.

And Fairmont wasn't just a search dog. He'd acclimated to being a house dog as if it was nothing at all new to him. Someone, somewhere, was missing him, either as a pet or as a working dog.

Helen. That was who needed to be my focus right now. Everyone said she was fine—or would be soon—but I needed to see it for myself.

Also, I was ready to tease out the details of this case from a handsome but somewhat close-mouthed sheriff.

"Yes," I said. "Absolutely. Let's go."

When we entered Helen's room, I was hit by how petite she was. She'd looked the same when I'd caught a glimpse of the paramedics removing her from the scene yesterday.

In the short but eventful time I'd known her, she'd been bursting with energy. She filled up the space she occupied, and her energy overflowed it. Usually.

Now she was pale, both her eyes blackened, and she looked fragile and small.

My eyes burned to see her in such a state.

She grabbed my hand. "I'm on some great drugs. Don't you even think for a moment that I'm feeling any pain."

I knew that couldn't be entirely true, but the fiction chased away my tears and made me smile. "I just can't believe this happened. You were only looking at posters, taking a few pictures, walking in your own neighborhood."

"I saw a little more than that," Helen said wryly. "The poster was tacked to the lamppost, but a little way down the sidewalk, Tim was riding his bicycle. Seeing them side by side like that had me wondering. I told you he was an odd child, didn't I?" She didn't wait for a reply. "Then I realized that we were in front of May's place, and it was Karen's day to clean there. And *that* jogged my memory that at least some of the pet owners used Karen Bishop's cleaning service. Suddenly, some of the puzzle started to piece itself together. Anyway, Karen saw me—just my luck she was bringing the trash can to the curb—and one look at my face and that was it."

"And she just brained you in the middle of the street?" I asked, baffled. There was nerve, and there was crazy.

"Well, no. She told Tim to head home and picked

up a brick from the Davenports' rose bed." Helen touched the side of her head tentatively. "And then she brained me."

Luke cleared his throat. "He must not have gone far, because it was Tim who interrupted Karen after she hit you with the brick."

"Really?" Helen frowned. "I don't remember that. Then again, I was probably out for the count at that point. I wouldn't have thought him capable. That's a brave thing for a grown man to do, and he's such a young thing."

"Yes, but it was probably him running away scared that helped you the most." Luke explained what he'd pieced together from the evidence and speaking with Tim. That after one blow with the brick, Karen had focused on hiding Helen so she could find her grandson.

"Well, that explains the scrapes and bruising on my legs," Helen said. "She must have dragged me all that way and up the drive to her car."

"Oh, I hadn't thought about that." I remembered Karen as looking strong, and she had toted some hefty boxes for me, but... "Wow. That's surprising."

"Adrenaline," Luke said.

"Truly?" I looked down when I felt Helen take my hand.

She squeezed my fingers. "Well, it's just about a miracle that I'm alive, then. But for a brave little boy, his well-timed flight, and a dog with an exceptional nose, I might not be sitting here in this attractive gown, looking forward to lunch in bed."

I wasn't sure that was true, but I let myself smile nonetheless, because she was here and, outside of the terrifying shiners she had, appeared to be in good health and spirits.

The blood trail Fairmont followed had been short, just a few houses from where Helen had been attacked. Luke and his men would have sorted it all out—but Fairmont had probably been faster. I took a breath. Best not to think about could-have-beens and might-haves.

Helen pulled the thin blanket higher so that less of that attractive gown was showing. If I had half her sense of humor in a similar situation, I'd consider myself a winner at life. She was an amazing woman.

"Luke," I said, "what do the pets have to do with everything? I feel like they're involved, but I don't understand how."

"They are, though not directly through Karen," Luke said. "Tim admitted to harming them."

"Oh," Helen said faintly. "I'd wondered. Not really, but...maybe?"

"I'm sorry about Ace, Helen, but we're sure that he and the other animals are gone." Luke exhaled. "He admitted to killing them and told us where he'd buried them. He even gave them gravestones, so once we knew the area to search, they were easy to find."

She nodded and looked a bit teary, but she didn't cry. I'd have sobbed till the tears wouldn't come, but that was me. Helen was made of tougher stuff.

"Why?" she asked. "And then to bury them with markers—why?"

I agreed with Helen. Why would a young boy do such a thing? A young boy who'd made a stand, brief though it may have been, against his grandmother when she'd been intent on harming Helen.

Luke pulled up a chair and offered it to me. When I declined, he sat down and leaned closer to Helen. Quietly, and with a glance in my direction, he said, "That's complicated. I'm not technically allowed to share this, so you ladies will keep this under your hats."

We both agreed.

"Tim's mother Jolene isn't dead." Luke rubbed the side of his neck. "She's currently incarcerated for murdering Tim's father."

"How in the blazes did Karen Bishop keep that a secret for all these years?" Helen's voice had ratcheted up in volume, so she peered over Luke's shoulder to make sure no one had heard her. Much more quietly, she said, "I would never have believed her capable of it."

Knowing what I knew of White Sage, I couldn't

believe anyone had kept a secret—a big secret—for that long.

"Oh my goodness," I said. "Georgie and Vanessa, they said Sylvester's murder was all about a secret."

Helen's eyebrows rose. "Met the dynamic duo, did you?"

Luke cleared his throat. "Actually, I've always considered you and May to be White Sage's dynamic duo."

Helen shook her head as if she couldn't believe the sheriff would say such a thing. But then I was pretty sure she winked at me. Maybe I'd imagined it, because she turned wide, innocent, non-winking eyes to Luke and asked, "How does Sylvester tie in to Karen's secret?"

"Sylvester knew about the murder," Luke said, "because he had worked with Tim. He kept the information private, exactly as his job required. Sorry, Helen, you may not have known, but Sylvester worked for Child Protective Services for a time."

"I did," Helen said, "but I'd forgotten."

Of course she knew. Helen had her finger on the pulse of White Sage, most especially the gossip.

Luke didn't look surprised. "No one in Sage County knew Jolene had murdered her husband because she lived a few counties to the west at the time, and Karen kept it quiet. Jolene was arrested, tried, and convicted there."

"No one ever heard a whisper about the murder? And they believed Karen when she claimed her daughter died, because who would lie about something like that?" I shifted closer to Helen so I could face Luke. "But that doesn't explain why Tim would hurt people's pets. What does Jolene going to prison have to do with that?"

"Right." Luke looked at both of us and seemed to weigh his options.

Very quietly, I said, "We already told you we would keep this to ourselves." I needed him to tell us, because I needed to know there was a reason for everything that had happened. The concept of closure had never sounded so necessary to me. And I believed that to be true even though I'd gone through a very unpleasant separation and divorce not so very long ago.

Finally, Luke nodded. "It seems Tim has been experimenting with death. He was young when his father died. It's unclear whether he was a witness or not—though I suspect he might have been. Minimally, he had knowledge of his mother's actions. Karen never got him help, not that we can find. After speaking with the boy, it's pretty clear he was forbidden from ever discussing or mentioning his father's death."

"But harming animals?" I said.

"I can't begin to understand the issues he's

dealing with, but I know that he told us he wanted to understand death, dying. I'm summarizing, but that's the gist. Beyond that, we'll have to wait to see what the psychiatrist says."

"That's horrible." I'd thought what a terrible situation Tim was in, having lost both of his parents, but this was so much worse. "I just can't believe that Karen wouldn't get help for him."

"I suspect that's the key to the murder case, right there. Sylvester must have found out about the pets and demanded that Karen do exactly that. We don't know that, not yet, but before she requested counsel, Karen admitted she was worried about losing Tim. She also mentioned that the 'quack shrinks' hadn't fixed her girl."

"The inference being that she sought psychiatric help for the daughter and, seeing no results, refused to send her grandson to a bunch of 'quacks.'" I considered my own experiences with therapy after my divorce. "It's also possible that the person who was supposed to help her daughter made her worse."

I'd been lucky on my third attempt, but my first two experiences with counseling—one psychologist and a therapist—I'd done my best to put out of my mind.

"Maybe," Luke said. "We'll see. She's going to prison for her assault on Helen, and I suspect she'll be looking to deal on Sylvester's death soon because we have forensic evidence from the scene."

Helen sighed and looked at me. "I feel terrible suspecting Sylvester of hurting Ace. He was a grumpy old coot. You didn't know him, but Luke will back me up." Luke nodded, and she continued, "But it sounds like he was trying to do the right thing, and that's what got him killed."

If that was the moral to this story, I was going to ignore it. I'd like to keep thinking that doing the right thing *wouldn't* get me killed. Except Sylvester hadn't just been killed. "She stabbed him in the heart with garden snippers. Who has that much anger?"

Helen squeezed my hand. "A woman who's lost her child to prison and is on the verge of losing her grandson to the system? Not that I would ever excuse such violence. There is simply no excuse. I can only think she was out of her mind."

Luke pushed his chair back and stood up. "Parsing her intentions and motives further is going to have to wait until she's willing to tell us more. And we may never know the real reasons for everything she did."

Helen nodded, and I could see she'd lost her perky spark. She was fading fast.

I gave her hand one last squeeze and said, "Rest

up. I'm sure all of those grandkids of yours will be by shortly."

"Yes, I'm ready for a nap." Helen shooed us out of the room. Luke and I were just about out the door when she called out, "Maybe you can take that woman on a proper date now, sheriff."

35

L uke didn't comment about "proper" dates or any other kinds as we walked back to his car. As he opened the door for me, he asked, "Are you okay? It's a lot to take in."

"I'm not sure how you do it. Every day you're dealing with people experiencing the very worst moments in their life." I shook my head. "You know, I met Karen. She helped me unload some boxes. She seemed so nice, so normal."

In retrospect, I could see that when she'd helped me unload my car, it hadn't been motivated by a simple desire for gossip. She'd likely been digging for facts on the case to try to determine if she was in the sheriff's line of sight.

Luke rested a hand on the open door. "You're right. I do see people in their most difficult times.

But that's when some people shine brighter. Like Helen." A sexy smile slowly appeared. "Like you."

My lips twitched, because I had hardly been at my best the last two days. But then I sobered, as I considered the flip side of that equation. "And when they don't shine brighter? When you see the ugliest side of people you've known most of your life?"

He sighed and his smile faded. "Look, if you're having the very worst day of your life, or even just an exceptionally bad one, say you find a body in your backyard"—he quirked an eyebrow at me—"maybe the guy who shows up to help can make that experience a little less terrible."

And he'd just made me see law enforcement officers in a new light.

"You, Sheriff McCord, certainly made my first murder a little less terrible." I leaned forward and kissed him on the cheek. "Thank you."

"You're welcome." He gestured to the interior of the car.

Once we'd both settled in for the drive back to White Sage, the conversation drifted to innocuous topics. Sally's was the best sandwich and soup shop, but in a pinch, the convenience store on Main actually had pretty decent sandwiches made fresh every day. They sourced their bread from Sally's baker.

And the state park was well worth the time to investigate. Fairmont was welcome on leash, the trails were well marked, and the native plants and trees beautiful at any time of year.

Also, the library could use some volunteers, if I was interested. Apparently, the books didn't re-shelve themselves, and staff had difficulty keeping up.

We covered some other topics—his mom's tiny home community, the best place for groceries—but not once did we discuss murder, assault, cadaver dogs, or the unfortunate end of the neighborhood's missing pets.

By the time we reached my street, my feelings for White Sage had settled firmly into the positive. I felt welcome and that new opportunities and friend-ships awaited me.

My feelings about the sheriff... Well, I decided I liked him quite a lot, even if he was younger than me, had a potentially dangerous job, and was related to half of the incredibly gossipy town I'd just moved to.

He pulled into my driveway and put the SUV in park. "I have to head into work now, but I was hoping you might consider that 'proper date' Helen mentioned."

Not that murder updates over lunch and impromptu breakfasts before visiting injured friends weren't lovely, but a lady eventually needed more. I was glad to see that Luke agreed.

"Are you asking me on a proper date?"

He grinned. "Most definitely."

Was I doing this? I'd already decided I liked him. But a date... I hadn't actually been on a date in... Hmm, best not to do the math.

Luke waited patiently for me to indicate my interest or lack thereof. And that sold me. Luke wasn't just kind, incredibly attractive, and easy to talk to. He was also patient. And I knew if I was going to venture into dating once again, I would be toe-dipping, not diving. I needed a patient man.

I nodded and then smiled. "Sheriff McCord, I would love to go on a date with you."

"Can I entice you with dinner and a movie, Ms. Marek?"

That sounded divine. And not least of all because there wasn't a single movie theater in all of White Sage. We'd be far removed from any towns-folk who might see us and revel in the affirmation that their sheriff was indeed "sweet" on me. I pretended to consider his offer.

"How about the drive-in? Fairmont can come, and it's three towns over." He grinned at me. "Not a single McCord on the staff."

Three whole towns over and no extended family connections. He was a mind reader.

And a dog lover.

Luke McCord might be just what I need. I wasn't

looking for forever. I wasn't even looking for right now. But Luke made it impossible for me to say no.

"It's a date, sheriff." I slid out of his car, gave him a final wave, then headed into my beautiful little box of a home, where my dog anxiously awaited me.

EPILOGUE

My lady is in love! I hope...

She's home, smells like my second favorite person Luke, and is smiling. A lot.

She says Helen is fine, and the bad people are caught. She also says a little boy is getting help that he needs. Her smile disappears when she talks about the boy, and her eyes shine with tears.

But then she tells me she has a date—I get to go!—and she's happy again.

She talks about filling the house, our home, with furniture.

And she whispers about a man—Luke, I think—who is kind and patient and maybe just right for now.

And finally, she tells me that she's happy. Here, in White Sage, with me, with her new life.

I curl up on the air mattress—it's quite a fine air mattress—and take an afternoon nap.

Ready for more of Fairmont and Zella's adventures? Their next story, The Scent of a Poet's Past, **is now available!**

Keep reading for two of Sally's recipes ("Bliss in a Bowl" Southwest Corn Chowder and Luke's Favorite Turkey Chili), several Fairmont-approved dog training tips, and an excerpt from The Scent of a Poet's Past!

EXCERPT: THE SCENT OF A POET'S PAST (PREVIOUSLY FAIRMONT FINDS A POET)

PROLOGUE

My new home brings me joy. My yard is filled with squirrels, my home with soft, warm places to rest, and my lady Zella spends her days showering me with affection.

My lady also has friends who bring me pets and treats and kind words.

Sometimes I miss my work—the thrill of the hunt, the smells I trained so hard to parse from all the other exciting odors in the world—but I love my life.

I love my Zella.

The hum of the grinding machine and the smell of coffee pull me from my bed. My breakfast is sure to follow.

CHAPTER ONE

Zella, I need you to find my poet."

I poured boiling water into my French press and flicked the volume on my cell a little higher. "I'm sorry—you need what?"

Fairmont pressed against my leg, reminding me that I hadn't filled his bowl yet.

"I've lost my poet, and I need you to find him." Geraldine McCord, the county sheriff's mom and my new friend, wasn't the sort to misplace her keys, let alone a human being. Fairmont's breakfast would have to wait another few minutes.

Geraldine might look like a cross between a hippie, a hiker, and an art teacher, but she was all business when it came to important matters—like losing people. If she said she lost her poet, there had to be a reasonable explanation.

Her voice held an edge of worry that was very unlike her. Picking my way through the few details she'd given me seemed a good start. "First, what poet?"

"My poet in residence. I'm sponsoring housing for ten days out of every month, and in exchange, the resident artist does outreach with either the high school or the local community while they're here." She huffed out an impatient breath. "I told you all about it. You said it was a great idea."

Geraldine owned The Hiker's Second Home, affectionately referred to as The Hiker by locals. The Hiker was a tiny-home community catering to both visiting hikers and local creatives. And she *had* told me about her Creative-in-Residence program, but only two or three days ago, and it had just been an idea at the time. How in the world had she managed to find a suitable candidate so quickly?

"Pablo is my first." She made a dissatisfied noise. "If this doesn't go well, there goes the program, dead before it's barely been launched."

I eyed the clock on my stove, but then gave in to the reality of my caffeine addiction and pushed the plunger on the press. Three minutes, five minutes—basically the same thing. "All right, so Pablo is your poet in residence, and he's gone missing?"

Complete silence followed my question, and just as I was about to ask if Geraldine was still on the line, she said, "Zella, did I catch you before your morning coffee?"

"No," I fibbed as I poured my first cup. "I'm just baffled as to why you're calling *me* if you truly believe one of your guests is missing."

"I would have called Fairmont, but he's not answering the phone, last I checked."

My favorite German Shorthaired Pointer lifted his head up and perked his ears. Seeing he had my attention, he trotted to the corner of the kitchen, nosed his empty ceramic food dish, then gave me a hopeful look.

Taking the hint, I quickly filled it.

"Fairmont is busy eating breakfast and isn't available to chat. Seriously, though, Geraldine, if one of your guests is missing, you have to call the police." Even as I said it, I knew exactly why Geraldine hadn't.

"Pfft. Bubba Charleston wouldn't be able to find my lost poet if there was a trail of gumdrops—or even beef jerky—leading the way. His only saving grace is that he knows exactly how useless he is and lets my son handle all of the real crime."

I'd only lived in White Sage for a few weeks, but it hadn't taken more than an hour as a resident for me learn that serious crime wasn't Chief Charleston's cup of joe. He'd ceded an entire murder investigation to Sheriff Luke McCord, Geraldine's son and my...ah, my...something complicated.

Not that I blamed the chief. From what I'd learned since moving here, the term "shoestring" didn't come close to describing his budget. It was more duct tape and rubber bands. The minuscule budget of the local policing force was one of the less attractive sides to living in a small town.

"When is Luke due back from New Orleans?" But I knew the answer before I'd even finished asking: not soon enough.

"Two more days. I could call him and have him come home early, but it's so rare for him to take a vacation that I hate to interrupt unless it's a real emergency."

"And you don't think it's a real emergency." I squeezed my eyes shut, inhaled the delicious aroma of my morning brew, and listened to the quiet crunch of Fairmont chewing the last of his breakfast.

"Not yet. But if you and Fairmont will just have a quick look around…"

She left the rest to my imagination.

Given Fairmont's history since I arrived in White Sage, Geraldine knew I'd have a hard time saying no. With one dead body, one blood trail, and a found missing person under his canine belt, Fairmont had developed quite the reputation locally.

I'd already turned down two cash offers to find missing cats. It had been heartbreaking, but I didn't trust Fairmont anywhere near an unknown cat and didn't have any idea how the two of us might go about finding a lost one.

Add to the equation the fact that Luke hadn't taken a real vacation in two years (as many helpful White Sage residents kept telling me, as if I were some lost soul pining for her mate in his absence), and I was feeling a tad pressured to cave to Geraldine's request.

"Why exactly do you think Pablo is missing and not just out for a stroll in the woods?"

"Oh dear." Geraldine took a breath. "I forgot to mention the blood, didn't I?"

Blood?

"How much blood?"

"A very small amount." When I didn't immediately acquiesce, she added, "A shaving accident's worth. And he didn't make it to breakfast. Pablo wouldn't miss a free meal."

Blood (not much, though), a missing tiny-home resident, and Geraldine convinced of Chief Charleston's incompetence. I winced, knowing my answer probably wasn't the right one, but I couldn't bring myself to say no. "Don't call Luke. I'll be over in twenty minutes."

"Thank you! You're an angel," Geraldine said. "I'll have a cup of coffee waiting for you."

I sighed as I disconnected the call. This would *not* end well. Either Fairmont would find a body— my spotted boy had a nose for death, quite literally —or he wouldn't. Either way, we'd end up calling Luke back from his vacation.

Hope blossomed as I considered one other alternative. Fairmont and I could take a nice stroll in the woods next to The Hiker and happen upon Geraldine's missing poet completely unharmed.

Except for the pesky question of the blood. And Pablo's disinclination to pass on a free meal.

Geraldine wasn't lacking in sense. If there was a

real question of harm to her poet, she'd have called the chief, no matter how little she thought of the man.

Wouldn't she?

As I transferred my coffee to a travel mug and snapped a leash to Fairmont's collar, I considered various harmless scenarios that resulted in minor blood loss.

By the time I loaded Fairmont into the Grand Cherokee, I'd convinced myself of Geraldine's theory. Pablo the poet had nicked himself while shaving. I'd also remembered that the trails near The Hiker weren't marked, and someone unfamiliar with the area might get turned around.

Never mind the fact that the "woods" next to The Hiker consisted almost exclusively of scrubby cedar making the cluster of buildings hard to miss, and most people didn't leave blood evidence after a shaving nick.

CHAPTER TWO

My lady is anxious.

I think she misses Luke.

Luke is my second favorite person, and he hasn't been to visit in days. That makes me sad, and I think Zella misses him as much as I do.

Maybe a car ride will cheer her up...

CHAPTER THREE

I cracked the rear windows on the drive to The

Hiker, and Fairmont moved from one side of the car to the other, his nose shoved into the two-inch gap as he tested the air outside. The sight of him enjoying such a simple pleasure made me smile.

The coffee I drank on the journey probably didn't hurt either.

By the time Fairmont and I arrived at The Hiker, we were both in good spirits. Fairmont adored riding in the car, and I'd decided that poor shaving skills and a bad sense of direction weren't so terribly unlikely.

Geraldine burst my good-humor bubble as soon as I pulled into the parking lot. She passed a glossy flyer featuring Pablo Navarro-Silva through the driver's side window.

A *full-bearded* Pablo Navarro-Silva, per his headshot.

There went the shaving theory. Clearly, Geraldine had been speaking metaphorically with the shaving accident comparison.

I tried to return the flyer once I'd exited the car, but she refused to take it. "Don't you think you should have a picture of him? So you can identify him when you find him?"

Since Fairmont and I weren't likely to run into any other heavily bearded men walking near The Hiker on a Wednesday, I had my doubts. But I folded and pocketed the flyer anyway. It was easier than arguing with her, and I needed both hands to attach Fairmont's leash.

Once I had Fairmont safely leashed, my cell phone stashed in my pocket (just in case a call to the police became necessary, which it wouldn't, but just in case), and my travel mug of coffee firmly in hand, I decided I couldn't really procrastinate further. "Let's have a look at his room."

Geraldine gave me the lowdown as we walked the path to the edge of the tiny community, where Pablo's cottage was located.

"I'm a little fuller than usual for midweek. I've got a writers' retreat group here now. They arrived yesterday."

Pablo the poet happened to be Geraldine's first in-residence artist, and there was a writers' retreat taking place now? Which raised the question... "I don't suppose you recruited Pablo from this retreat group?"

"I did. It seemed too good an opportunity to pass up. When I saw Paul's—Pablo's—name on the list, I took a chance he might be interested." Geraldine leaned close and nudged me. "He's from White Sage originally. Well, originally from North Sage Grove, but he spent most of his childhood in White Sage."

The bearded poet, who clearly hadn't nicked himself shaving, also had ties to the local community. My confidence in finding Pablo wandering in the woods unharmed nosedived. Ridiculous, really, because White Sage had welcomed me with open, friendly arms. The town was a little gossipy, yes, but generally it was a lovely place populated by good people. The missing man having a history with the town shouldn't mean anything.

And yet my unease grew.

Fairmont's cold nose nudged my hand. I stopped to fondle his velvety ears. Was it my imagination, or was Fairmont nosing the air more than usual? One dead body under my belt and I was becoming paranoid. Then again, one really was enough to make any normal person a little wary.

Geraldine pointed to a tiny stone cottage just ahead. "That's where Pablo's staying. I switched his cottage assignment after he agreed to take the in-residence spot. That way, he wouldn't have to move after the retreat had finished. The stone cottage is where all the in-residence artists will be staying."

I knew that cottage. I'd overnighted there several weeks ago when I'd found a dead body in my yard and Luke had kicked me out of my house for the night. The décor was quite firmly pink.

"Hopefully his masculine sensibilities weren't offended by the color scheme."

Geraldine smiled. "I sent him pictures, so I assume not. Paul never was one to fuss over a free ride. Sorry, I mean Pablo. Authors and their *noms de plume.*" She rolled her eyes. "He was Paul Winston when I knew him. He changed his name to Pablo and took his mother's maiden name when he left White Sage."

Interesting. The timing of his name change made me question if he was reinventing himself for a new life or hiding from his old one.

Or neither of those, my more practical side offered. Maybe the name change didn't mean anything at all. I'd ask him when we eventually interrupted what was likely the poor man's morning commune with nature.

"Shall we?" I asked.

Geraldine nodded with a grim look in her eye.

As we approached the cottage, Fairmont's demeanor changed. His gait became more animated, his attention fully occupied by the little stone house. I had to remind myself that he'd followed a blood trail with equal enthusiasm and that had been just a few scattered drops.

But even with that thought in mind, by the time we reached the front door, my unease was off the charts.

CHAPTER FOUR

I smell it.

Death.

And a metal tang in the air: blood.

I can taste the coppery traces on the back of my

tongue. Blood has many notes—old, new, tainted—but it is always blood.

The catalogue of scents in my head is big. Bigger than my words. Bigger than what I see with my eyes. Blood is blood. Death is more complicated. I know there is the scent of a recently dead and the scent of a long dead, but there are so many scents in between.

I recognize this death odor easily.

A recently dead smells almost like a person, and that's what I catch in the air now.

There is also the smell of a man. The man smell mixes with the scent of recent death.

Excitement zings through my body, and I feel ready to burst from my skin.

I hesitate.

Zella doesn't like dead bodies.

My lady doesn't like death. She doesn't like blood.

But when I work, she always tells me I'm a good boy, so...

To keep reading, pick up your copy of Fairmont Finds a Dead Poet!

SALLY'S "BLISS IN A BOWL" SOUTHWEST CORN CHOWDER RECIPE

I'm only giving you this recipe in hopes you'll make it and impress that gorgeous new lady friend of yours. You said she's trying to eat a little healthier, so I'm giving you a vegetarian option. Don't mess it up—the recipe or your chance with Zella.

Love you! Sally

PS: I idiot-proofed it, so follow the instructions. I mean it. Seriously. I'll withhold your personal Sandwich Shoppe delivery service (Annie's agreed) if I find out you messed this up.

INGREDIENTS

- 2 medium potatoes, peeled and diced. (medium = no bigger than your fist)

- 3 cups corn kernels, frozen, not canned. (kernels = not on the cob)
- 1 medium onion, diced. (diced = cubed, preferably no bigger than a nickel though the potatoes can be closer to a quarter)
- 1 red bell pepper, seeded and chopped. (Chopped is coarser than diced. And, yes, I know, it's like a foreign language, which is why I'm providing definitions. Best. Sister. Ever.)
- 1 green bell pepper, seeded and chopped. (seeded = remove the stem and seeds and put in your compost bin. You still have a compost bin, right?)
- 1 rib (that's like a stalk) of celery, chopped
- 4 cups chicken or vegetable broth. (Organic vegetable broth in the carton is best. Ask Harry at the local grocery if you're confused.)
- 2 cups heavy cream. (Substitute full fat coconut milk from the can if you're going for the vegan option.)
- *1 jalapeno, minced. (minced = as small as your big, clumsy man-hands can chop)
- 2 cloves garlic, minced. (Buy a "bulb" of garlic, then detach 2 of the smaller "cloves" from the bulb. Still confused? Text me, and I'll send a pic.)

- 2 tablespoons extra-virgin olive oil
- 1 teaspoon cumin. (That's a spice, buddy, so check the spice aisle at the grocery.)
- Kosher salt (taste first, then add **only if needed**) and freshly ground pepper

HOW-TO

1. Find the big pot, the one I gave you three Christmases ago. Stainless, heavy, holds about 8 quarts. (If you lost it or gave it away, I will haunt you after I die.)
2. Add 2 tablespoons extra virgin olive oil to the large pot, then turn the burner to medium high. Wait till it's hot. (Smoking is bad; just look for it to shimmer in the light). Once hot, add your already diced onions.
3. **Do not leave the kitchen!** No watching sports or doing laundry. Keep an eye on the onions, moving them around in the pot a bit until they're soft and kind of translucent. Better yet, set a timer for 5 minutes, because it shouldn't take longer than 5 minutes to achieve onion transparency.
4. Now, pay attention, because time is short for this one. Add the minced garlic (and

maybe jalapeño, see note below), and cook an additional **2 minutes** while stirring. Much more than that and you're looking at scorched nasty bits in the soup. Again, **do not leave unattended.**

5. Pat yourself on the back, you're almost there! (Unless you've burnt everything, in which case, stop watching football, throw it in the trash, and start over).

6. This is the fun part. Chuck all this stuff in the pot: chopped bell peppers (red and green), the corn kernels (frozen or thawed; you're good either way), chopped celery, diced potatoes, cumin, and the organic veggie broth.

7. Increase heat from medium-high to high until the whole pot is boiling. (Do I have to explain boiling? Ha! Just kidding ☺)

8. Once boiling, reduce heat to low and let everything simmer for 30 minutes. Set your oven timer, but that's an estimate. Your test to determine if it's cooked long enough is if the potatoes are tender. You should be able to stick a fork into a potato chunk and it almost falls apart.

9. Stir in coconut milk, then sample before you add salt and pepper. (Remember, Zella can always add more salt, but she

can't take it out once you've dumped in a
quart of the stuff.)

10. Best enjoyed while hot—not scalding.
    Don't burn her pretty mouth, because we
    all know you've got plans for those lips.
    Okay, that might have been a step too far.
    Now I'm thinking about my brother
    kissing a girl. Yuck.

11. Enjoy!

*Use judiciously. If Zella likes spicy, you're good. If
she likes a little spicy, use half. If she's not from
Texas and thinks bell peppers liven up a meal, then
skip it.

LUKE'S FAVORITE TURKEY CHILI RECIPE

I'm so excited you want to try my Turkey Chili recipe! This is a slow cooker version of the menu recipe. Not that I think you can't manage the original, but I'm hopeful you can teach my brother how to make this one. (That man is not *handy in the kitchen.)*

He'll love the slow cooker version just as much as the original, I'm sure. Although, honestly, Zella? You could cook him just about anything and he'd be tickled. Anyway... Here it is!

Hugs, Sally

MAKES: Enough for one large, hungry law officer, his date, and a small, lunch-sized serving left over, or (in normal-people language) 4 servings!

INGREDIENTS

- 1 lb ground turkey
- 1 medium yellow onion, diced
- 1 red bell pepper, seeded and diced
- 1 yellow bell pepper, seeded and diced
- 2 cloves garlic, minced
- 28 oz tomato sauce, 1 can
- *15 oz black beans, 1 can, drained and rinsed
- *15 oz pinto bean, 1 can, drained and rinsed
- 1 c. frozen corn, thawed
- 2 tsp chili powder
- 1 tsp ground black pepper
- 2 tsp kosher salt

OPTIONAL INGREDIENTS

- 1 jalapeño, sliced
- ¼ c. fresh cilantro, chopped
- 2 Tbsp green onion, sliced

And the nitty gritty...

1. Combine the following ingredients in your slow cooker: pound of ground turkey, diced onion, diced red and yellow peppers, minced garlic, can of tomato

sauce, beans (black and pinto), thawed corn, chili powder, pepper, and salt.

2. Set the crockpot for low, and plan to cook for about 6-8 hours. Alternatively, you can cook on high for 4 hours, but it might not be quite so flavorful.

3. And that's it—just garnish, and you're done!

I'm pretty sure, with a little coaching, even my brother can manage this one. So maybe you can invite Luke over, and you two can make this one together? (Hint, nudge, etc.) Luck, and thanks for feeding my favorite (okay, only) brother. ~Sally

Without going into the whole debate—is it really chili if it has beans?—I'll just say that I've made it both ways and Luke likes it with ☺

FAIRMONT-APPROVED DOG TRAINING TIPS

We all know that Zella doesn't speak canine. But if she did, I'm pretty sure this would happen...

Tip #1

Fairmont: *Treats are wonderful. You should give your dog lots of treats.*

Zella: Maybe the dog should do something good before he gets a treat?

Fairmont: *I guess...*

Zella: Because when you give a dog a treat or scratches or pets, you're basically telling him he's a good at what he's doing or just did is good...right?

Fairmont: <sigh> ... <head tilt, sad look> ... *But I like lots of treats.*

Zella: You're a very good boy, so you have plenty of opportunities to earn treats.

Fairmont: <stubby tail wag>

Tip #2

Fairmont: *Dogs should be allowed in the kitchen, with the people and the food. People are wonderful, and food is wonderful, and people and food together are especially wonderful.*

Zella: But what if the dog jumps on the table?

Fairmont: <blink>

Zella: I know you're too gentlemanly to jump on the table.

Fairmont: <blink> <blink>

Zella: While I'm watching.

Fairmont: <stubby tail wag, canine grin>

Zella: How about this? Polite dogs who don't beg, jump on the table, drool excessively, or otherwise act inappropriately are allowed in the kitchen.

Fairmont: *I'm not sure. I got lost halfway through the list.*

Tip #3

Fairmont: *Human beds are softer than dog beds. You should let your dog sleep on the human bed.*

Zella: So...you know I love you.

Fairmont: <raises eyebrows>

Zella: And you're welcome on the bed.

Fairmont: <stubby tail wag>

Zella: But you shed.

Fairmont: <ears droop>

Zella: A lot. You shed a lot.

Fairmont: <lies down with chin on the floor>

Zella: You're welcome to keep sleeping on the bed—not *in* the bed, but *on* it.

Fairmont: <lifts head hopefully>

Zella: I'm just saying, not everyone wants their shedding dog to sleep on the human bed.

Fairmont: *But it's soft and high and smells like you.*

Zella: I get it. But it's not for everyone. Also, I don't think that counts as a dog training tip.

Fairmont: *Human training tip?*

Zella: <sighs> You win.

The story ideas that survive to be written are the ones that nag until I decide they aren't going away. This story was different, because at its heart is Fairmont, and Fairmont's character was based on my dog Vegas. (He was never a cadaver dog, but I'm certain he would have rocked that job if he'd had the opportunity...and a decent trainer.)

I started this story about four months after Vegas passed, and if you read the dedication, you know that I cried quite a bit while writing it—more than I've ever cried while writing a story.

I didn't debate whether to start Fairmont Finds. I just wrote it. In fact, the series was supposed to be something else altogether, but as soon as I started typing, it was clear I was going to write about the coolest dog I've ever known. He had the kind of personality that made him loved by many, and I hope a few more people will get a chance to know him through my Fairmont character.

Thank you for reading this story and for letting me share some of my memories of Vegas with you.

ABOUT THE AUTHOR

When Cate's not tapping away at her keyboard or in deep contemplation of her next fanciful writing project, she's sweeping up hairy dust bunnies and watching British mysteries.

Cate is from Austin, Texas (where many of her stories take place) but has recently migrated north to Boise, Idaho, where soup season (her favorite time of year) lasts more than two weeks.

She's worked as an attorney, a dog trainer, and in various other positions, but writer is the hands-down winner. She's thankful readers keep reading, so she can keep writing!

For bonus materials and updates, visit her website to join her mailing list: www.CateLaw-ley.com.